Lucky Duck

Lucky Duck

CHRIS KURTZ

art by Jennifer L. Meyer

Clarion Books
An Imprint of HarperCollins*Publishers*

Clarion Books is an imprint of HarperCollins Publishers.

❈

Lucky Duck

Text copyright © 2024 by Chris Kurtz

Illustrations copyright © 2024 by Jennifer L. Meyer

Library of Congress Control Number: 2023937486
ISBN 978-0-06-331134-3

The artist used pencil, ink and digital techniques
to create the illustrations for this book.
Book design by Alison Klapthor
23 24 25 26 27 LBC 5 4 3 2 1

First Edition

To Enaiyah, who brings me joy.

❧ Chapter 1 ❧

Being a duck is the best thing ever. I know that because I'm already ten days old. Hatching is excellent! Actually, come to think about it, busting out of that shell is a lot of hard work. It was finally *being* hatched that was so great. Getting my legs down under my body instead of hiked up around my head was a huge relief. I could hardly move inside my egg. Couldn't change positions. Heck, there wasn't even enough room to change my mind!

When I finally kicked myself out, I just lay there beside my shell pieces and tried to gather my strength. And as soon as I could, I stretched and stretched. These stretches and first breaths of sweet, clear air made all the work of hatching worth it.

"Frank, my dearest," said my mom. "Welcome to the world!"

My family is the best family ever. I have the best mom ever and the best life ever. Anyone who isn't a duck . . . I feel a little bit sorry for them.

And my mom is teaching us stuff every day.

"Ducklings," she says this morning, "I have something to tell you."

I'm under her wing with my siblings. We aren't listening

because we're too busy messing around. I'm nipping at my sister Darlene's toes, and my brother Darryl has snuck around behind and is pulling my tail, and we're laughing and carrying on.

"Stop carrying on," says my mother. "Come out from under there and pay attention."

My sister bites me good on the leg.

"Hey, that hurt," I say. "I'm gonna get you back."

"Ouch!" Mom stands up in a flutter of feathers. "Somebody just bit me on the leg! Stop that, you three, and come out where I can see you. Whoever bit me is in trouble!"

We can tell when Mom isn't playing around, so we

come out. Luckily for me, Mom doesn't make us say who bit her. Instead she has us sit in a row with Darlene in the middle so Darryl and I will stop messing around. We look at her and we can tell that this moment is extra important.

"You probably don't know this," she begins, "but you three are my very first hatchlings. I've never, ever hatched ducklings before." She stops and looks at us. We look at each other.

"The most special thing of all happened on the day I decided to incubate you three," she says. "Incubate means I started keeping you warm. I was walking back to the nest when I found an amulet, and I knew I would be successful this time. It was—"

"What's an ambulet?" says Darryl.

"Amulet, not ambulet," says Mom. "An amulet is something that comes to you when you don't expect it. . . . It takes care of you. My amulet was a little white stone with . . . guess how many little dark spots on it."

"Three!" I shout. "I bet it had three little dark spots!"

Mother laughs, which makes me feel wonderful. "Yes, Frank. Three dark spots on a little white stone. And I will keep it forever."

"A lucky stone," breathes Darlene.

"Say 'amulet,'" says Mother.

"Amulet," we all say. Except I'm pretty sure that Darryl still says "ambulet."

"Yes," she says. "I always watch for amulets that might bring good fortune. Children, always keep an eye out for them."

I make a promise to myself to be an expert amulet finder.

"Where's the amulet that brought the good luck of us?" says Darlene, which is exactly what I was thinking.

I start poking around the nest. "Did you hide it after we hatched?"

"I didn't hide it exactly," says Mom. "I just put it in a safe place. See if you can find it."

"Found it!" says Darryl. He pulls the little white stone out from under the nest.

The three of us crowd around Mother's amulet. It's beautiful, and we all want to look at it and peck at it. After a moment she steps in and pushes it back under the nest.

"Since we are your first ones, that makes us special, doesn't it?" asks Darlene.

"Yes," says Mom. "Very, very special."

"How special?" says Darryl.

"Indescribably special," says Mom, and she looks so happy.

"Did you ever lay eggs before?" Darlene asks. "That didn't hatch?"

I can see right away that Darlene shouldn't have said anything about that. Mom's happiness seems to disappear like the sun when a cloud passes over it. "Yes, I did," she says. She blinks quickly a few times, and then she turns her neck and tucks in a stray feather.

I wish that Darlene didn't ask that question, but it was the very same question I wanted to ask.

When Mom turns back to us, her eyes are sad. "I had two batches of eggs before you, and they didn't survive. So I'm extra *extra* happy that—"

"She didn't have a lucky amulet," says Darlene to Darryl and me.

"What happened to the other eggs?" says Darryl.

Darlene gives him a big shove with her wing. "Shut up, Darryl," she says. "This isn't a good time."

"What, so you can ask questions but I can't?" he says.

"Darlene is right," Mom says. "This isn't a good time."

Darlene squints at Darryl.

Mom ignores it. "No sad thoughts are allowed today because today is special. Every first-time mother duck gets to have her own celebration called a Duckanalia. I've invited your aunties and uncles to my Duckanalia today."

"What happens at a Duckanalia?" says Darryl.

"Other ducks in our clan gather around and say nice things and congratulate the mother and officially welcome the ducklings into the clan."

"Will there be any other ducklings?" I ask.

"Nope," says Mom. "Just adult ducks."

"If you ask me," Darryl says, "it sounds really uncomfortable and awkward." Darlene and I nod.

"Well, this is how ducks do things. Everything will be fine and it won't take very long. Your aunties and uncles are coming, so I want you to be on your best behavior. They are going to just love you!"

Darlene and Darryl and I just stare at each other.

Mom waits until we look at her. "I want to see a good attitude from all three of you." She taps her left foot to show us she's serious.

"It'll probably be nice," Darlene mumbles.

Mom looks at Darryl and me.

"It'll probably be nice," we mumble.

"Thank you, children," says Mom. "That's better. Now help me clean up this nest."

We walk around and pick out the loose sticks and feathers from our nest. I totally don't think it will be nice, but I can tell that Mom is excited. Hopefully, her friends will notice how strong and good-looking we are. And hopefully someone will notice that, actually, I'm the strongest . . . and probably the best-looking of the whole batch!

We spend the rest of the morning preparing, and before too long we hear a loud quacking coming our way.

"Quick, everyone into the nest," says Mom.

Pretty soon these great big auntie ducks come pushing through the reeds.

"Ladies, I'd like you to meet my new family," says Mom. "Sit up straight, Darryl and Frank," she whispers.

Darryl and I sit up straight.

"Samantha, they're just beautiful," one lady duck says to my mom as if we can't hear her. The big auntie ducks make a circle around our nest, pushing each other a little bit so they can see.

"You were so dedicated," says another lady duck. "Sitting there on those darned old eggs day after long day."

I look at Darryl and grimace because I don't like being called a "darned old egg," and he grimaces back. Two of the auntie ducks climb up the side of our nest and start nibbling softly at the tops of our heads.

"They are just darling," says a third. "All that hard work was worth it, Samantha, you poor dear."

"Just look at that fuzz all over their little bodies. They're so adorable!" And the comments keep coming. More aunties climb in, and I have to move over so I don't get walked on.

"Look at those little heads."

"Don't those too-big beaks look adorable? Is it true that an amulet came along at just the right time? You're so lucky."

Then a large uncle duck pushes his way through the reeds around the nest. "Samantha, you're a queen among hens, an absolute queen!" He has a really loud voice. "I heard you had a doozy of a time waiting for your little brood to finally decide to peck their way out."

I have to scramble again so I don't get stepped on. Pretty soon I'm on the edge of the nest, and I can't even see Darryl and Darlene anymore. The big drake steps into the nest, and the aunties jump out to make room for him.

Darryl and Darlene and I slide into the middle. Mother steps in and nudges us forward.

"Thank you for coming, Uncle Dave," says Mom. She whispers to us, "Say thank you, children."

"Thank you, Uncle Dave," we mumble.

Uncle Dave stares at each one of us from close range, starting with Darlene and coming down the line to me. "It was a small clutch," he blares, "but three for three is what we were hoping . . . HOLD IT!" This time he shouts so loud I jump.

He pushes his big beak into the side of my head.

"Hey, I think we have a problem!" he yells. "Where did this one come from?"

I shrink back as close as I can to Mom.

All the auntie ducks come over and stare at my face. And then big Uncle Dave takes his big old yellow beak and donks me. Right on the head! *Donk, donk.*

"Hey," I say. "That hurts!"

"Stop that!" Mom yells. "What are you doing?"

"That one's not ours." The big duck starts backing up because my mom is chest to chest with him, pushing him.

"I don't accept that one into the clan," he is still yelling.

Mom is smaller but it doesn't matter. She is shoving Uncle Dave backward. The auntie ducks are scattering.

"He. Most. Certainly. Is. Mine!" Mom bumps Uncle Dave on each of her words. The auntie ducks all start quacking at once. "Out of my home!" Mom shouts. "Out of my family circle! I didn't invite you here to insult my family. Out! This Duckanalia is over."

The big uncle duck and all the auntie ducks scramble out through the reeds. We can still hear Uncle Dave shouting after they're gone.

I rub the top of my head. "What just happened, Mom?" I ask.

"Don't worry about that." Mom nudges us into our nest. "Don't even think about it, dearies. They won't be invited back." But she doesn't join us. Instead she paces outside of our nest.

Darryl and Darlene just sit there, staring first at Mom and then at me.

"Stop staring," I say. "Say something or do something, but don't just sit there and stare."

"Whoa," says Darryl.

"Yeah, whoa," says Darlene. "That was so weird."

"Mom," I say. "What—"

"I said don't think any more about it." Mom stops pacing. "Time for your nap, children." She steps into the nest and uses her wings to brush us under her, and for once I don't complain.

But I can't sleep because I keep thinking about the head donking. So I think about the lucky white stone with the three dark spots instead, resting below us under the nest. Protection. Mom is my amulet, I think to myself.

Chapter 2

The next day, Mom has a big announcement. "Today is the day for your first swim."

Wahoo! Darryl and Darlene and I jump up and down and bump into each other until we fall out of the nest onto the ground. Then we dance in a circle, quacking our heads off. When we get dizzy, we flop down on our backs and watch the sky spin around.

"Everyone flex your feet," says Mom.

Darryl and Darlene and I wiggle our toes upside down and compare paddle feet.

"Oh my goodness," says Mom. "You three are so silly! Darlene, your little feet are adorable."

"What about me, Mom?" says Darryl. "Are my feet adorable?"

She leans down and nibbles the bottoms of Darryl's feet. "Delicious." She laughs.

"What about me, Mom?" I say. "What about my feet?"

"Your feet, Frank . . ." Mom steps over to me, and I wiggle my feet even more. Darryl and Darlene stand up to look.

"Your feet are huge, Frank!" says Darlene.

"Yup," says Darryl. "Definitely not adorable or delicious.

In fact, I think you might have stepped in some poop."

I stand up. "I did *not* step in poop," I say. "Mom, are big feet good?"

Mom puts a wing on my back. "When it comes to webbed feet, big is fantastic," she says.

"See?" I say, and I give Darryl a little kick in the side with one of my fantastic big feet. "Too bad your feet aren't fantastic, only delicious. The fish will probably eat your delicious feet. You'll be so sad and footless."

"Frank, no kicking," says Mom.

"Mom." Darryl walks behind Mother because I'm glaring at him. "Do fish eat duck feet?"

"Of course not," she says. "But mother ducks do!" And she snaps her beak and then lunges at our feet. We all quack and squeak and flap our wings and run in circles, trying to escape.

Mom suddenly stops chasing us and gives us the side-eye like she might start up again, and I hope she does. But instead she says, "All right, children, you're too fast for me. I'll have to nibble on your feet some other time."

"Can you please chase us again, Mom?" asks Darlene.

"Please!" Darryl and I say.

Mom ignores us. "You have a swimming lesson, children. Webbed feet make ducks the best swimmers of all birds."

I look down. The paddles at the ends of my legs are giant!

They are definitely bigger than Darryl's and Darlene's. I can tell swimming is something I am going to be really good at.

"This is gonna be the best day of our lives!" I say.

"This will be the second-best day of your lives," my mom says.

Darryl and Darlene and I look at each other, and our eyes get wide. Whatever she's going to say next sounds really important.

"Ducks are born to swim like mosquitoes are born to buzz." Mother bends her neck over one wing and slowly pulls a long feather over her beak. "But the day you take flight . . . that will be the best day of your lives, trust me."

"Wahoo!" I jump up and down and flap my skinny little wings, which have a lot of fuzz but zero feathers. Absolutely nothing happens. No lift whatsoever.

Darryl rolls around on the ground laughing. "You were not flying at all!" he says.

"It takes more than just wings to fly," says Mom. "It takes practice, and something else. You need *flight* feathers. See these?" She spreads her big, beautiful wings. "The long feathers that come off the ends of your wings are flight feathers. That's what you need to fly."

I don't care who laughs. I flap my wings again. Darryl laughs at me again. But pretty soon he and Darlene are flapping around with me just for fun.

"All right, enough carrying on," says Mom. "Everyone

get in line behind me and follow me down to the pond."

"Do you think we might find a lucky amulet on the way to the pond?" I ask from the back of the line.

"Are you on a quest to find an amulet?" asks Mom without turning her head.

"Yup," I say, even though I don't know for sure what a quest is.

"Mom, what's a quest?" asks Darlene.

"A quest is when you really want something," I jump in.

Mother stops and turns around. "A quest is a long and difficult search for something important. Something special."

"I'm definitely on a quest," I say, and I look into the bushes on both sides of the path. I would love to find something important.

When we get to the pond, Mom doesn't stop. She just slips right in and expects us to follow her. Darryl and Darlene slide in behind her but not me. I have an idea.

"Ahhh! I'm scared!" I pretend to be all nervous. "What if I can't swim?"

"Frank, you're a waterbird." Mom swims back to help me. "Just jump right—"

"Just kidding!" I shout, and I leap and make the biggest splash I can.

"Okay, Frank," says Mom. "Stop playacting."

Darlene has the idea of ducking her beak into the

water, so I try it too. Pretty soon we are putting our whole heads underwater and splashing each other and carrying on. Mom doesn't seem to mind. "Stay close," she says. "We'll be getting out soon, before you get chilled. When your feathers come in, they'll keep you warm. They're not just for flying."

I can't explain how good water feels to a duck the very first time. It's like hatching all over again. It's like the sweetness of taking your first breath, only now it's my whole body that's breathing.

"When will our feathers come in?" I swim up to Mom fast and try to make her think I'm going to run into her. She doesn't even flinch.

"Your feathers will grow in when it's time," she says. "You just make sure you're a strong and deserving bird when they come."

"You mean deserving duck, right, Mom?" I say. Because I don't need to have feathers to know that ducks are the best birds ever.

"Okay, sweetie." She pats me on the head. "Just be the best you can be."

"Plus I'm going to find an amulet, *and* I'm going to go on a quest!" I tell her.

"A quest, Frank?" says Mother. "You're pretty young to go on a quest. What would you be searching for on your quest?"

"Something important," I say. "Something so important it helps everyone."

"You're important just by being yourself," she says. But to me this sounds like something every mother says to her ducklings.

I swim over to see what Darryl and Darlene are doing. They're zigzagging, so I join in and we zigzag around and I bump into Darryl on purpose.

"Ahhh, I'm wounded," he says, and starts swimming in a circle like he's hurt.

"Stop playacting," I say.

"I want to do that," says Darlene. "Frank, bump into me!"

I do and she starts acting hurt and swimming all wobbly.

"Frank, are you being nice?" calls Mom.

"We're just playacting, Mom," says Darryl. And we keep on like that until I get bored and decide to hide from my siblings behind some reeds.

But while I'm hiding, something makes me turn my head. I think I hear someone say, "Hey, c'mere." I look around but I can't see anyone. Darryl and Darlene paddle off, and it looks like they've stopped playing the game.

I'm sure that pretty soon Mom is going to say she doesn't want us to get chilled, and I do *not* want to think about getting out. In fact, leaving this beautiful water behind seems like the worst thing ever. So I stay out of sight behind the reeds.

The next thing I know, I'm in the middle of a group of half-grown ducks.

"Hey, are you that oversized egg kid?" says one duck with a feather that sticks straight out of the back of his head.

This is my first chance to talk to someone besides my own family without my mom being right there. Lucky for me, these guys seem really friendly.

"Hi, guys," I say.

"What are you doing?" says the duck.

"I'm on a quest," I say, even though I had completely forgotten about my quest. But I hope it sounds important.

"He's on a quest," says the first duck to his friends. Then he says to me, "Are you on a quest to be normal? You know your brother and sister hatched out three days before you, right?"

"I didn't know," I say. This is the first I've heard of it.

"Wow," says the one girl duck in the group. "A late hatcher. Oversized egg, oversized head. You probably have oversized feet."

"Yeah, I do!" I say. I try to show them, but my feet won't lift out of the water.

"Well, everyone is talking about you." She comes up close and rubs the top of my head with her wing tip. "Nice fuzz. We're so lucky to get to hang out with someone as special as you."

"Thanks!" I say.

"You didn't tell us your name," she says. "Can we just call you Big Head?"

"No . . . ," I say.

"How about Fuzz Butt, or FB for short?" says a duck with a dark spot on his beak.

"No," I say. "My name is—"

"How about just weirdo," says the duck with the feather sticking out from his head.

"My name is Frank!" I say.

The duck with the dark spot on his beak says, "My mom told me nothing good is ever going to come from a big old oversized egg. It will either be scary or disappointing."

"Like possibly a reptile," says the fourth duck. He's the smallest and still has a little bit of fuzz around his neck.

"I'm not a reptile," I say.

"My mom said she couldn't wait to see what was going to come out of that big old egg," says the girl duck. "She just knew it was going to be weird."

"I'm not weird," I say. "Watch this!" I swim really fast in a circle. "I'm practicing to be the best duck I can be."

"Yeah, that's not gonna happen. We have something we'd like to show you," says the duck with the feather sticking up. "You might be a good swimmer, but you're never gonna be—"

"Frank!" I hear my mother. She comes barreling up out of nowhere. "I've been looking everywhere for you."

The teenage ducks scatter, and I can see why. Mom looks mad. "Who were you talking to?" she says.

"Those were my friends," I tell her. "They were going to show me something."

"Those were not your friends," says Mom. "And I told you to stay close."

"Bye!" I wave to the teenage ducks, who are swimming together again. They don't wave back.

"Time to get out," Mom says. "Darryl and Darlene, come get out. NOW!" She still sounds mad, which is really confusing.

Darryl and Darlene swim up and climb out of the water, grumbling, and all three of us follow Mom up the path to our nest. "Why did we have to get out so soon?" says Darryl.

"We were having so much fun," says Darlene. "Where were you, Frank?"

"I was making friends," I say.

"Frank!" says Mom. She stops and faces us. "I already told you, those were not your friends. Now hurry up." She turns around, and we have to run to keep up with her.

"They *were* my friends," I whisper to Darryl and Darlene. "They were going to show me something, but then Mom made us get out."

When we get back to the nest, Mom scoops us all under her warm body to take a nap. Darryl and Darlene are snoring away in no time, but I'm not sleepy. I poke my head out between her wing and her body.

"Mom," I say, "was I a late hatcher?"

"Shh," she says. "You were a perfect hatcher. And you are off to a great start with your swimming. You're going to make me proud and show everyone what a great bird you are." She starts to hum a song.

"You mean duck, right, Mom?" I say.

"Yes, duck." Mom nibbles the top of my head.

"Mom," I say again, "was I an oversized egg?"

She stops humming. "You were a beautiful egg. Remember the three dots on my amulet stone? You were destined to be my third dot. Now, no more questions. Go to sleep."

"I love you, Mom," I say. I bring my head back under her body, and I breathe in the smell of my mother. I'm glad she doesn't think I was an ugly egg. "I'm going to make you very proud of me someday," I whisper to myself. "It's my quest."

❈

The next morning, I wake up as soon as Mom stands up and steps off our nest. The sun is bright and the sky is blue. I watch as she shakes her tail and turns her neck to preen a few back feathers. Before I can think of something to say to make her stay, she steps through the reeds and disappears. When I stand up, Darryl and Darlene snuggle together, still asleep.

Mom is probably just going off for a bite to eat or an early morning swim. I miss her already, and I think about quacking really loud so that she comes back. But I don't. I want to do something that will make her proud of me. I decide to clean up.

"What are you doing?" says Darlene when I take a leaf out from under her.

"Sorry," I say. "But the sun is up and it's clean-up-the-nest time."

"It's never been clean-up-the-nest time before," grumbles Darryl.

They don't get up to help me, so I continue tidying up on my own. I find four pebbles, and I turn them over carefully to see if one might be an amulet. But none of them is special in any way.

When Mom comes back, she looks around. I can tell she notices when she nibbles the top of my head. It makes me so happy! Our pond is fresh. Our air is clean. The sky is blue. And ducks are the best. What a lucky hatch! Being a duck is excellent. It's easily the best thing ever.

"So how are my sleepyhead ducklings this morning?" Mom steps up into the nest. "What a clean nest!" She nibbles the tops of Darryl's and Darlene's heads, which makes me feel a little bit jealous. I manage to not say anything. "Did you two get so tired from cleaning the nest up that you had to go back to sleep?"

They didn't even help one bit! I want to scream. But I keep my beak shut. I want Mom to see that it was me who cleaned up, so I rush over and snap up a stray leaf and toss it out of our nest circle. But Mom is straightening her feathers and doesn't even notice. Darryl and Darlene still have their eyes closed like they want to go back to sleep.

"Yesterday we took our first swim," says Mom. "But I

mentioned that the day you take flight will be the most exciting day of your lives. It takes strength and practice even before your flight feathers come in. Who's going to show me their wing flaps?"

"Me, me! I will!" I jump up and down.

"Have you been practicing?" she asks.

Practicing? I didn't even know we were supposed to be practicing. "Yes! Yes, I have!" I lie. "I want to show you how much I've been practicing."

"Okay," says Mom. "Show me."

I climb down out of the nest and flap my wings as hard and as fast as I can. I look at Mom, and she doesn't seem like she's very impressed. So I flap even harder and I hop up and down. I try to flap my wings three times before my toes touch the ground. I only stop when I'm exhausted.

"Very nice, Frank," says Mom. "Now who *else* wants to show me their wing strength?"

Darryl opens one eye.

"Darryl?" asks Mom.

He shuts his eye again.

"Mom," I say, "can I show you my paddling strength?"

"Have you been practicing?" she asks.

"Yup!" I say. It's another lie.

"Frank, how can you practice paddling without water?" she says.

Oops. I have to think fast. "Like this," I say. I flop down

on my back and stick my legs up in the air. Then I paddle my feet as hard as I can.

That brings a big laugh from my mother. It is the sweetest sound ever. "Oh, Frank," she says. "You look absolutely ridiculous!" And she laughs her silvery laugh again. I paddle even more because her laugh is like sunshine on the water and I don't want her to stop.

"Zoom!" I say. "Zoom, splash, zoom, splash!"

Still laughing, Mom steps over and nudges me to my feet with her beak. Darryl and Darlene are awake now too. They are looking at me from the side of the nest. Mom puts a wing on my back. "Frank, you wear me out. But someday you will make your mother very proud."

My heart skips a beat. Proud? I just made my mother laugh and it was a sweet feeling. But what if she was proud of me? Now I want more. "Mom, I want to make you . . ." But I don't finish because Darryl and Darlene choose this moment to finally jump out of bed, and they crowd around Mom.

"Mommy, are you proud of me?" says Darlene.

"Very proud," says Mom.

"Are you proud of me, too?" asks Darryl.

"Of course I am." Mom steps backward because Darryl and Darlene are pushing at her.

I just watch. Mom didn't say she was proud of me like

she did with my brother and sister, and part of me feels jealous.

"Come on, everyone." Mom turns around and starts walking. Darryl and Darlene are still jumping around her and bumping her. "Let's go for a morning swim together."

I spend the whole way down to the pond thinking about how I'm going to make my mother proud. I've already showed her what a good swimmer I am. I try to think of something more, but nothing comes to mind. I'm also thinking about my duck friends that Mom didn't want me to talk to. I wonder if I can sneak away and find them again.

My chance comes so easily it surprises me. Mother seems distracted today and swims over to talk with her friends. Darryl and Darlene look like they don't quite know what to do. Not me. I head straight for the clump of reeds where my teenage duck friends were hanging out last time. They seemed so nice yesterday and they might have some advice about how to make my mom proud of me. Anyway, they said they had something to show me.

Sure enough, the minute I go behind the reeds, there they are. It's as if they knew I was coming.

"Hi, guys," I say. "I was hoping I would find you."

"Hey, it's the oversized egg kid," says the duck with the sticking-up feather. "We've been waiting for you."

I'm pretty sure I don't want to be called the oversized

egg kid, but I ignore it. "You've been waiting for me?" I say. I can't believe how lucky I am. "I'm just glad I knew where to find you."

"Oh, we're not too hard to find," says another duck. "The four of us always stick together. We call ourselves the Fab Four Quackers. If you want to find us, just look for four ducks who were normal-sized eggs and hatched after twenty-eight days—which is when ducks are *supposed* to hatch."

"Oh," I say. "If you guys could use one more duck to make it a fivesome, I'd love to join you. Then we could be the Fantastic Five Quackers!"

"Nah," says the girl duck. "We're good, right, guys?"

The other ducks nod.

"So," she says, "are you questing today?"

"No," I say. "I don't have any ideas for a quest yet. I want to make my mom proud. Do you guys have any ideas?"

"Lots of ideas," says the first duck, with the sticking-up feather. He sort of seems like the leader of this group. "Although, I gotta say, not hatching at the normal time makes it a challenge."

"Well, I'm up for a challenge," I say.

He swims around behind me, so I have to turn in a circle to watch him. "We've been so rude, not introducing ourselves. You're probably wondering what our names are," he says. "My name is Normal Duck." Then he starts pointing to the other ducks. "This over here is Average

Duck. That is Regular Duck, and right here"—he points to the girl duck—"she is Typical Duck."

"Oh," I say. I'm not sure why they keep making such a big thing out of me hatching late, but maybe if I keep being friendly they'll be friendly right back. "My name is Frank."

"Cool," says the first duck. "We can call you Freaky Frank."

"No," I say. "Just Frank."

"Or just Freaky," says Normal Duck, though I'm pretty sure that's not his real name.

He swims a little too close and I try to back up, but all the other ducks are crowding me from behind. They stare at me, and they have a funny look in their eyes. "Those don't seem like your real names," I say. I'm starting to feel really uncomfortable, and I want to swim away, but I'm surrounded.

"If you want to make your mom proud of you, I have a suggestion," says Normal Duck. "Disappear. Just walk away and get lost because you are weird. And mothers don't like children who are weird."

I turn in a circle, looking for a way to get going. Mother was right—these are definitely *not* my friends. "I'm just going to go now," I say.

"Hang on," says Regular Duck. "Don't you remember that we said we had something to show you?"

I'm absolutely sure I don't want to see what they have to

show me. I keep trying to push out of their circle, but they keep blocking my way.

"Come on, guys," says Regular Duck. "Let's show him what we have ready for him."

And then, all of a sudden, they start donking me on the head. I try to escape. I go this way and that way, ducking and twisting, but it's no use. I feel trapped. It's as if they know where I am going to go before I even make my moves, because my way is blocked each time and the donks just rain down until my ears are ringing.

Then suddenly they stop.

"There, that wasn't so bad, was it?" says Regular Duck. "That was just a test to see if you have quality."

"Quality?" I say. The top of my head is aching. "That hurt. And it didn't seem very friendly."

"Hey," says Normal Duck, "we're your *real* friends. We don't do that for just anyone, you know. By the way, my real name is Derrick."

"And my name is Dennis," says Regular Duck. "You did great. Didn't he, guys?"

"I'm Dexter," says Average Duck.

"And my name is Donna," says Typical Duck.

"So I won't have to go through that again?" I say.

"Never again, little buddy." Derrick rubs the top of my sore head. "Sorry about that, but it was necessary."

"Whew," I say. "That was pretty terrible."

"Well, don't get too comfortable," says Derrick. "Because there will definitely be other tests. Or maybe even a quest. But if you're cool, you'll be perfectly fine."

"Okay," I say. I'm not too sure about more tests. Unless they help me be the best duck I can be. Then I might be interested. "Well, I gotta go find my mom."

"Yeah, about that," says Donna. "Don't go blabbing to your mom about the test."

"Yeah," says Dennis. "If you blab around, then the test doesn't count."

"Frank?" I can hear my mom calling me.

I push my way between them and then turn around. "I'll see you guys later."

I swim as fast as I can. I paddle hard until I come up behind Mom.

"Oh, there you are, Frank," she says. "We were looking for you. Come on now, time to get out."

✖

That night in the nest, I start thinking again. I think so hard I can't sleep. I poke my head out from under my mom's wing. "Mom," I say.

"Shhh," she says. She's looking up. "There's the moon. It's beautiful."

I follow her gaze. The moon is big and round. Very nice, but it doesn't solve my problem.

"Mommy, those teenagers . . ."

"Shhh. You're not really looking," she says. "Let the moon speak to you. Let your mind go to the dreaming place."

I look at the moon again. I see that it is duck-beak yellow. I notice that it seems like it gets closer the more I stare at it, but when I blink, it gets far away again.

"The moon speaks to all ducks," says Mom. "Can you hear it?"

All ducks? It speaks to all ducks? I listen very carefully and wonder if this is another test. I hear the stream. I hear the wind. I hear the frogs and a fish splash in the pond. I don't hear the moon. I want to hear the moon, but I don't.

"Yep, I sure can," I lie.

"The moon is our mother," she says. "Mother Moon swims through the sky and calls to her family. You can feel her call in your heart."

Mother tucks her head under her wing. I keep my head out from under my mother's warm body and listen some more. Maybe the moon only talks to grown-up ducks.

I am just about to squeeze back inside and let sleep take me away to the dreaming place when I hear it! I can hear the moon! It's speaking to me!

I feel my heart start pounding. It is a faraway honking

that makes my wing nubs tingle. I can tell there are words . . . something about flying . . . and a journey, but I can't quite make out the rest. But I can almost feel my flight feathers growing, and in my mind I see myself flying through the night air. The honking sound gets gradually softer and softer until it fades away completely, but I can still feel the soft touch of the moon on my head.

❋❋ Chapter 3 ❋❋

A few days later, Mother calls us to go down to the pond. "Special lessons today, children."

We follow her into the water.

"I've noticed that your feathers are starting to grow in," says Mother.

We look around. Sure enough, I see tail feathers and wing feathers on my brother and sister. Then I look behind me. Nothing on my tail except gray fuzz. No feathers on my wings, either.

Darlene giggles. Darryl points a feathery wing at me and starts splashing around and laughing.

I squint at Darryl so he knows for sure that he's got a good head donking in his future if he keeps this up.

"Not everyone develops at the same rate," says Mother. "But duck feathers set us above all other creatures—animal or bird. They shed water, they allow us to fly, and they are beautiful. Ducks are the handsomest of all birds."

"Hooray!" My brother and sister flap their wings and dance in a circle. I flap my wings too, and I hope like crazy that my feathers will start growing in really soon.

"Lesson number one."

We get quiet and watch Mother.

"We ducks are most at home in the water, but we are special because we are comfortable on land, amazing in the water, and superb in the air."

"Yippee!" Now I'm catching the spirit. I can tell that duck lessons are going to be a lot of fun, and I can't wait to be a grown-up duck.

"Ducks are super fliers! Flap your wings seven times."

Flap, flap, flap. I flap my wings *ten* times, splashing everyone around me.

Just then I hear a sound that almost makes my heart stop. It is the moon talking again. I look up. The moon is just a pale sliver in the blue sky. I look at Mother to see if she heard it, but she is still talking about flying.

It is such a faraway beautiful sound that at first I wonder if I imagined it. My wing nubs start to tremble, and I look straight up over my head. A flock of birds is flying over us, far above.

They sound just like the moon.

Their voices make me feel all shivery inside. My wings flap again all by themselves, and I start swimming in circles. And then suddenly the faraway birds are gone.

I look around to see if anyone noticed. Darlene is cutting her eyes sideways at me, but Mother is still teaching. Maybe she was concentrating so hard on the lesson, she didn't even hear the birds. I shake my head to clear it.

"Ducks are excellent divers, too," says Mother. "Lesson number two, children: Duck your heads. Deep breath. Bottoms up!"

I duck my head and make sure to hold my breath just a little bit longer than everyone else. Darlene tries to stay under as long as me, but she can't.

"Lesson three," says Mother when we pop back up. "Ducks don't take kindly to non-ducks in our pond, and we are naturally suspicious and we do not talk to them. Intruders are met with group action, and a duck bite is surprisingly strong." She swims by each one of us and stares into our eyes. "Let me see you practice. Show me your surprisingly strong bites, children!"

My brother and sister snap their beaks all around. I snap my beak. Darlene swims in front of me. "You don't belong here," she says, "and I am naturally suspicious."

"Oh yeah?" I say. "Well, I'm naturally suspicious of

you too. Bring your head over here, and I'll show you just how naturally suspicious I am."

Mother interrupts. "Lesson four, preening. Watch me, children, because to be a good duck, you must know how to preen." She turns her head and nips and nibbles at her wing feathers almost like she's eating them, but not really. I look behind me at my fuzz, and I pretend to preen my feathers.

Mother shows us how she works her feathers one by one to fix any strays. My brother and sister look at me and giggle. I decide to ignore them this time.

But Mother paddles around behind me. "Frank?" she says. "I think I see some tail feathers poking out?"

I turn in a circle to see. That doesn't help much, though, so I look at Mom. "Are they really coming in?"

"Where?" says Darryl. "I didn't see anything."

"Come take a look," says Mom.

Darryl and Darlene go around behind me. This is super embarrassing, but I stay still, just hoping and hoping.

"Yup," says Darryl. "I can see them too." He sounds a little disappointed.

I crane my neck around again, but I can't see anything but fuzz. Mom seems like she's the most excited. "Frank, once your feathers start coming in, you won't believe how quickly it will happen!"

I'm so happy I race off, pushing a big wave in front

of me and making foam in my wake behind me. After I get tired, Darryl and Darlene and I practice preening our fuzz together. But pretty soon they get bored and start swimming in circles and watching the little whirlpools they make behind them.

Not me. I am going to be the best duck ever, so I keep preening my soon-to-be-feathers fuzz. Then I go bottoms up and hold my breath as long as I can. Then I flap my wings and swim back and forth till my legs burn. And then I snap my beak surprisingly strongly.

❁

The morning is sunny and warm. I can hear the other ducks in the duck village quacking.

"Time for breakfast," says Mommy. "I'm going to teach you to look for snails."

"Yippee!" says Darryl.

"Wahoo!" Darlene flaps her wings excitedly.

I flap my wings too, even though deep down I'm not so sure about snails. So far all Mom has shown us to eat is bugs. And I really, *really* don't like bugs. Every single one has tasted terrible, though Darryl and Darlene act thrilled every time they swallow a grasshopper like it's the best thing ever. To me grasshoppers taste like dirt only crunchier.

I'd rather eat grass. Grass is delicious. I tried some. . . .
I don't know why but I just wanted to, and it tasted *so good*!

I do it secretly, though, because I don't see anyone else getting excited about grass and I don't want anybody to think I'm weird. Or freaky.

Probably snails will be yummy. Yep. I tell myself they are going to be my favorite.

We trail each other to the edge of the pond and slip into the cool water. There are ducks everywhere. I look around for Dennis and his friends. The pond is Fab Four free.

"This is the best duck pond ever, and we have the best snails," says my mother. "That is why our duck clan has always been on this pond and always will be." She swims over to some really tall reeds. "These are cattails. Look for the snails—fat little black dots on the stems of the cattail reeds, just under the water line."

I see one and I dash over to snap it up. Darlene sees it at the same time, but she isn't as quick as me. Well, actually she is quicker, but she doesn't bump as hard, so I get the snail.

A second later, I wish I had let Darlene beat me to it. Turns out snails are crunchier than grasshoppers at first but then mushier, and they taste even more like dirt.

While I'm trying to rub the sticky snail goo off the top of my mouth, one of my uncles swims up and mistakes my head for a snail. *Donk, donk*, right on the noggin.

"Hey," I say. "Watch where you're pecking!"

Donk, donk. "Clear out of here, squirt."

"I'm not a squirt," I say, but I back off. I look for Mother to help me, but she is busy showing Darlene where the next snail might be. I pay attention so I know where *not* to look.

The uncle duck swims toward me as if he is going to donk me again, so I paddle off as fast as I can to catch up with Mother. The donking gives me a headache. The grown-ups seem to think snails are only for them.

Which is fine with me. I hate snails! But I don't like getting pushed around.

I see Darlene find a snail and snap it up. I notice that there are aunties and uncles around her, but no one is donking *her* on the head. "You have a wonderful duckling there," an auntie says to my mom.

I look around and still don't see my Fab Four friends anywhere. I decide to pretend I'm looking for snails over in a spot where the water is warm and shallow. Probably there are no snails here, which is why there are no uncles or aunts for me to worry about either. I stir up the mud as if I'm hunting for bugs, and I hope I don't find any.

Out of the corner of my eye, I watch Darlene and for a minute feel a tiny bit sorry for myself. Then I see Mother, and I know everything will be fine.

One of these days very soon, she'll be proud of me and think I'm the best duck kid ever.

Where the water gets shallow, there is a smooth rock that looks good for standing on, and so I stand on it.

Then I hear a voice.

⁂ Chapter 4 ⁂

"What are you doing?"

I look around to see who is talking to me. My family has drifted out of sight. There is no one there.

"Down here."

I look down. Nothing but the rock I am standing on. Then the rock blinks.

"Ahhh!" I shout, and jump-flap off. "Who . . . what are you?"

"I'm a turtle," says the rock. "What are you doing here?"

"I live here," I say. I look the turtle rock over because I've never seen one before. Could this be an intruder? It was definitely pretending to be a rock. That might be an intruder thing. Maybe it is trying to be sneaky.

I lower my neck and advance on it, hoping I look scary. The turtle rock blinks again, but it doesn't move. I give it a good donk on its back with my beak, which works out pretty much like you might think it would . . . which is that it hurts me more than it hurts the turtle rock. So I move up and donk it on its ugly little head.

"Ouch," says the turtle rock. "That hurt. Why did you do that?"

I feel bad now because it didn't even try to swim away

or fight back. "I thought you might be an intruder," I say. "I'm a duck, and ducks have always been on this pond and always will be. Ducks don't like intruders. So . . . what are you doing in our duck pond?"

The turtle rock just blinks. "You don't look like a duck to me," it says.

"Okay, so I'm not a duck yet," I say. "I'm a duck*ling*. Big deal. Do you have a name?"

"Ummm." The turtle rock's head moves slowly to one side then to the other. It might be thinking. "Not exactly. The clutch of eggs I was in had eleven boy turtles, fourteen girl turtles, including me, and only four duds. That's too many hatchlings to give everyone a name. Plus, my mom didn't raise me."

"What?" I say. "Why didn't your mom raise you?"

"I raised myself," says the turtle rock.

I don't know what to say about that. I feel a little bit sorry for this turtle rock for having such a careless mother.

I decide to change the subject because I don't want to hurt the turtle rock's feelings. "So . . ." I look around in case I'm missing something. "Where are all your brothers and sisters of this amazingly big family?"

"I don't know. They're probably still in the little swampy place where we all hatched out. But I like ponds. So I came here." The turtle rock turns its neck and looks at me with one eye. "We're not a close family."

"Well, you're in a duck pond now where pretty much all the ducks are like one big family. And around here everyone has a name," I say. "It's no good not having a name. We should give you one." I think for a bit. "I know, we could call you Turtle Rock, or TR for short."

TR blinks at me.

"Do you like it?" I say.

She doesn't answer right away. I wait.

"Is that the best you could do?" she says finally.

"For now," I say. "It's cute. Or we could call you No Name, but that would be pretty sad. We can definitely choose something better than No Name."

"Since I raised myself, I might want to pick out my own name," she says.

"Oh," I say. "Whatever."

"Intruder!" The scream comes from behind me. It's so loud I jump. TR jerks her head inside her shell in a flash. Even her feet disappear.

I spin around in a circle, looking for the intruder. "Where?" My heart is pounding.

"Right there!" My sister is shouting. She is looking at TR's shell. "You were talking to it!"

"That's not an intruder," I say. "I already checked. That's a turtle rock."

"Don't you know anything?" my sister asks. "That's a non-duck and non-ducks are intruders! I'm telling Mom that you were talking to an intruder."

"Well, you scared it into its shell now," I say. But I feel bad. Maybe a good duck would have chased a turtle rock away.

Darlene swims off, probably to tell Mom. What a blabber beak. Now I could be in trouble. I'm pretty sure Mom won't be feeling proud of me today. I can't stand the thought of facing her disappointment in me.

I rap my beak on TR's shell. Nothing. "TR?" I say. "You can come out now. That was just my sister." Still nothing. I know I could wait for her to come back out, but now I feel confused. I wonder why I wasn't scared. Maybe I'm brave. Or maybe I'm just weird.

·⅏⟶ Chapter 5 ⟵⅏·

After waiting a little longer for TR to come out, I follow Darlene. I'm still hungry, but I can't think about anything except what Mom will think after Darlene tells her what I was doing. When I join my family, Mother doesn't say anything about how long I've been gone. All she says is "Time to get out, children."

She shoos all three of us out of the water. Then she says something that makes my heart sink like a stone. "Darlene and Darryl, you go on ahead to the nest. I need to speak with Frank."

Darlene gives me a look, and I'm pretty sure I know what's coming. I watch my sister's feathery tail disappear and wonder when mine will look like hers.

Mother waits until I'm looking at her. "What's this I hear about you talking to a non-duck?" she says.

"Not a *dangerous* non-duck, and not an intruder," I say. "A friend." A friend? I don't even know what made me say that. "I mean . . . a turtle. It was just a friendly turtle. Mom, can we just go now?"

"Samantha!" Big Uncle Dave is storming up the path. "Samantha, I've been looking for you. I've called a meeting," he shouts. He always shouts.

"Oh, good morning, Dave!" says my mom in a super-cheerful way that I know is fake. "I'm in the middle of family time. Is this something that can wait? What is the meeting about?"

"It most certainly *cannot* wait," shouts Uncle Dave. "And it isn't something we can discuss in front of the little ones," he says in a slightly lower voice, as if I can't still hear him perfectly well. "We have a non-duck problem!"

"A non-duck problem?" Mother looks straight at me. "Well, let me get my ducklings into their nest and I'll be right there."

Now I'm pretty sure I'm in trouble. She turns around and I follow while Uncle Dave goes storming off back down the path, shouting at the next duck about the meeting.

"Frank," Mother says without looking back. "Please come up and walk beside me." I run to catch up.

"Weren't you listening when I told you not to talk to non-ducks?" she asks me without slowing down.

"I was listening," I say. I try to breathe hard and talk at the same time, which isn't easy. "Am I in trouble?"

Mom slows down a little. "Don't you want to be good?" she asks me.

This question hits me right in the heart. I want so much for her to be proud of me. "I *do* want to be a good duck," I say. It's the truest thing I've ever said.

Instead of Mother telling me that I need to try harder or reminding me about the rules again, she just looks at me . . . like she doesn't know what to say.

"What?" I say. "Why are you looking at me like that?"

"I was just thinking about the day you hatched," she says. Her voice has gotten soft again. "One of the best days of my life."

"Mom, I don't get it," I say. "It was just a little turtle."

Mom sighs. "I can't explain it any further. We ducks are just naturally suspicious and easily alarmed."

I don't know what to say. I want to be a good duck, and it feels really bad to know that I'm not one. "I'll do better next time," I say.

"I know you will, honey." Mom swishes her wing feathers lightly across the top of my head. "Hurry and walk straight back to the nest. I need to go back down to the meeting." She taps me on the beak and says as I pass by, "Don't. Go. Anywhere. Till I get back."

Mother hurries down the path, and I stand there watching even though I know I should be headed to the nest.

As soon as we're all settled in the nest together, Darlene says, "Frank, I'm really, *really* sorry. I didn't know. . . ."

I don't say anything.

"Frank," says Darlene, "did you hear me? I said I was

sorry. Do you forgive me?"

I'm still mad at her for telling on me, so I don't answer. Instead I jump up and step to the edge of the nest.

"Frank!" shrieks Darlene. "Where are you going?"

I've never left the nest on my own before. "I'm going to follow Mom," I say. I don't even know why I say this. I just know I can't sit in this nest, waiting for bad news.

"Frank, you can't," says Darryl. "Mom said to stay right here."

"I know," I say. "But I have to find out what's going on."

I can still hear them calling my name as I run to where Mom disappeared. A few steps later I think maybe this isn't such a good idea. But if I am going to be in deep trouble, I just have to know what everyone is saying.

I race down the path. For once I am certain that Darryl and Darlene won't be following me. I know I'm *really* breaking the rules now . . . after I already broke them by talking with TR.

I don't have to go as far as I think before I hear loud talking. It's big Uncle Dave. He has to be the loudest duck in the whole world.

"Samantha, this is a matter of utmost importance," he is saying.

"Now, Dave, let's be sensible. . . ." My mom gets drowned out in a hubbub of quacking and complaining. There must be a whole group of ducks. I tuck in behind some tall grass

so I can hear everything.

Uncle Dave quacks louder than all the rest and quiets them down.

"I'm glad you want to be sensible, Samantha, because it is the council's most sensible members who, in the interest of safety and protection, have made the rules that—"

"Dave," my mom interrupts him, "it was just a turtle. A grass-eating, hardheaded little turtle. So I don't know what sort of protection you think we need from a turtle."

I'm surprised to hear Mom say this. It is just what I

would have said. The group starts quacking again.

"I am not talking about a turtle! Everyone listen!" Uncle Dave shouts over the noise, and everyone gets quiet. "Listen very closely." His voice gets softer and I move closer. "Sister Velma has informed me that two of her ducklings have disappeared."

There is a gasping sound from inside the tall grass.

"They were behind her on the way down to the pond," Uncle Dave continues. "Sister Velma heard a sound and turned around, and her little ones were gone. She thinks it was . . . and I told her it couldn't be, but she feels quite sure it was a fox."

There are more gasps, and for some reason I get the shivers, and I've never even seen a fox.

"Quiet please!" Uncle Dave shouts. "Drakes and hens, listen carefully. Keep a lookout for amulets of protection, everyone, and do your part!"

There is another commotion of loud quacking. Uncle Dave shouts something more, but the council is getting louder and louder.

I turn to run back to the nest, but then I see my mother charging up the path toward me. "Frank," she calls, "I thought I told you to stay in the nest!"

I hustle back home ahead of her and hop up and in with Darryl and Darlene.

But Mother doesn't follow. She paces back and forth outside our nest.

"What's happening?" Darlene whispers to me. "Is this about the turtle?"

"No," I whisper back. "There's a fox."

Mother stops pacing. "Children, look at me." When we are all looking at her, she takes a deep breath. "It is my job to keep my ducklings safe. There is a fox in the area. A predator. Do you understand me?"

I nod. Mom looks at Darlene and Darryl and they both nod.

"So we are *not* going to go down to the pond right now. We are *not* going to explore or practice. And I am *not* losing any of my ducklings to a fox like poor Velma did." She stops and takes another deep breath. "And my instincts tell me we need to move our nest."

"Our home!" Darlene jumps up and screeches. "The only home we've ever known?"

"Darlene." Mom looks full-on at her. "It's just a nest, okay? So you can stop being so dramatic."

"But I just love our home so much," Darlene whimpers. "And this is the home where the lucky amulet protected us."

"Yes, it is the only home you've ever known, which is part of the problem. It smells like a duck home, which is exactly what a fox would be looking for . . . or smelling for.

So we are not staying here. I'll come back for the amulet later. Right now I have too much to tell you about, and I can't talk and carry it in my beak at the same time."

"My instinct says we have to bring the amulet with us right now," says Darlene.

"Darlene," says Mother. "That's a feeling, not an instinct. There's a difference. Now let's go."

We all stand up, and I jump out of the nest. My brother follows me.

"What's an instinct?" I ask Darryl.

But Mother hears my question. "An instinct is when you know something without even knowing how you know it." She nudges Darlene out of the nest.

I look at Darryl again. "Do you get that?" I ask. He shakes his head.

"I don't either," I say.

Darlene peeks under the nest. "Bye, amulet. We'll come back for you."

"Now stay extra close," says Mom. "And all eyes wide open, alert for danger."

Darryl and Darlene and I look at each other, and then we check all around in the grass. But mainly we stay really close to Mother.

"What exactly do foxes look like?" I ask.

"Taller than me," says Mother. "Reddish-yellowish fur and big teeth. But while we're at it, keep a lookout for all kinds of predators, like raccoons, possums, and weasels."

"What do they look like?" Darlene asks.

"Raccoons are large with dark spots around their eyes. Possums are about my size. Both raccoons and possums are family destroyers. They love to eat eggs and hatchlings. But they're slow and sneaky, and they can be chased off by an alert duck. Weasels and their kin, on the other hand . . ." Mother shakes her head. "Half the size of a possum but twice as dangerous."

"What do you mean, their kin?" I ask.

"Weasels have bloodthirsty relatives," she says. "Martens, minks, ferrets, and stoats. But they all really like to eat little ducklings who don't stay close to their mother."

We stay so close Mom almost steps on us a few times. Then she stops in the middle of a stand of tall grass. "Perfect," she says, and begins to walk in a circle, flattening the grass wherever she steps. "This will be our new nest."

We watch as she starts building up the edges of the nest. As soon as we get the idea, Darryl and I bring her dried grass and sticks that we can reach without going outside the circle that Mom has flattened out. Darlene tries to copy Mom, tucking sticks and grass here and there.

"How did you learn how to build a nest?" she asks.

"Instincts," says Mom.

"This new place feels really hidey," says Darryl.

"Yes," says Mom. "That's the idea."

When the nest is finished, us three ducklings jump in and get comfortable.

Darlene slowly scooches close and then leans into me. I know it's her way of saying she's sorry for getting me into trouble. Mom climbs in and puts her wing over us, and we stay in the new nest the whole day.

But the night feels different, sounds different. And Mother doesn't tuck her head under her wing. I know she's listening. Listening for the fox.

⚶ Chapter 6 ⚶

The next day I find my Fab Four friends again. It would be an exaggeration to say that they are excited to see me. In fact, when I swim up and say hello, no one even looks my way. That seems sort of good because it probably means I won't be getting tested. But bad, too, because I would like to make some friends.

"Hi, guys!" I say. No one turns around. They are floating in a tight little clump with their heads in the center, and there is a lot of talking. I lean in so I can hear what everyone is so excited about.

Someone says, "Feathers everywhere, like snow on the ground."

And then someone else says, "And one of them wasn't even eaten. Just killed for nothing, not even food."

That's when I figure out that they're talking about the fox and Auntie Velma's babies.

"That's what I heard too," says another duck. "And I heard they got their throats ripped out. Can you imagine what it's like to have your throat ripped out? You'd be like—"

And suddenly a duck bursts out from the middle. It's Derrick. He's thrashing and splashing around. The whole group breaks up and watches. Someone starts laughing and then everyone is laughing. Then Derrick stops thrashing and flops his head sideways to show he's completely dead now. He drifts in a slow circle.

"Bravo!" Donna says.

"Good dying," I say, because I want to let everyone know that I'm here. Derrick snaps his head up. He is very much not dead, and he swims a little too close to me, which makes me back up.

"Hey, guys, look, it's Freaky Frank." Derrick bumps into me. "He's coming to check on the performance. How was it, Freaky Frank?"

"It . . . it was fine," I say. "But I thought, after I passed the test, you weren't going to call me that anymore."

Derrick looks at the others as if he can't remember for sure.

"Remember?" I say. "After you donked my head really hard?"

"I'm pretty sure I remember," says Dennis. "Was it something like this?" He rushes at me like he's going to donk me again.

"Hey," I say, and I cover my head with my wing and start to swim away.

"Just kidding!" he shouts.

I stop and come back.

"Jeez, can't you even take a joke?" says Dexter. "It was a joke, just like the dying duck routine."

"That's pretty funny," I say, even though I don't think it's funny at all.

"So . . . speaking of dying ducks," says Donna, "did you hear the news about Auntie Velma and her . . ."

"Yeah, I heard," I say.

"We were just wondering who might be next," says Dennis. "Could be you."

"Or it could be you," I say.

"Or . . . he might have a taste for something weird like you," says Dennis.

"Or something stupid like you," I say. I start backing up in case I need to swim away in a rush.

But Derrick swims in between Dennis and me. "Hey there, big guy. I'm glad you showed up, because everyone has to find a way to be of use in a time like this."

I stop backing up because it seems like maybe we might not be fighting anymore. But I'm not sure. I like being called "big guy," though, that's for sure. Derrick comes up and puts a wing over my back, and I let him. But I'm ready to paddle out of there at top speed if it looks like I might get donked on the head again.

"We ducks have to pull together in tough times. And this is a very tough time." Derrick's eyes lock with mine, and he swims us into the middle of the group. I relax a little. "Right, guys?" he says, and turns to the other ducks.

"Sure, Derrick, anything you say," says Dennis.

"What's on your mind, Derrick?" says Dexter.

"Well, we can't expect the grandpa and grandma ducks to do everything, right?" says Derrick. "I mean we all have to do our part."

Donna swims closer and Dexter and Dennis follow. They don't try to surround me, so I don't feel like I need to get away. In fact, everyone has serious looks on their faces. And Derrick brushes his wing over my head in a way that seems really friendly.

"So do you think there is a way for me to be useful?" I ask.

"Extra useful," says Derrick. "Not every duck can be as useful as you. Did you ever notice that your feet are a little bigger than some ducks'?"

"Kind of," I say.

"Special," he says. "And did you notice that your head is a little taller than other ducks your age?"

I nod.

"Special." Derrick paddles backward a few strokes and looks me up and down. "Doesn't that make him special, guys?"

"Super special," says Donna.

"And special ducks get to do special things." Derrick swims back up to me.

"What kinds of things?" I ask. I definitely like where this conversation is going. Now I'm really glad that I met the Fab Four and passed their test.

"Remember your quest?" he says.

I nod.

"Some ducks are so special they get to go on a quest," says Derrick.

I start to feel light-headed. This could be my chance.

"In case you didn't notice, there is a big problem on this pond." Derrick starts swimming back and forth in front of us. "In case you didn't notice, there is a predator, a fox, preying on our families."

"I noticed," I say.

"And in case you didn't notice . . ." Derrick goes on as if he didn't hear me. Donna, Dexter, and Dennis are watching him just as closely as I am.

"In case you didn't notice," Derrick repeats, "special times call for special heroes. And you, Frank, could be just the hero we've been waiting for."

I can hardly breathe. I could be a hero? I look at the Fab Four and they are looking at me. I stop myself from swimming in an excited circle and take a deep breath. "What do I have to do? And what's a—"

"Frank," says Derrick. "What is the first thing a duck does when there is danger?"

I think for a minute. "Call a meeting?"

"Okay, I guess you're right. But what's the second thing a duck does in an emergency?"

"I guess I don't know," I say.

"They fly," says Derrick. "They fly away. Do you know why the ducks on this pond aren't flying away?"

I shake my head.

"Because it's hatching season." Derrick starts paddling back and forth again. "And all the young ducks like us can't fly yet."

"Oh," I say. "So . . . everyone is staying because of us?"

"Unless," says Derrick. "Unless someone goes on a quest to save us. All of us."

"I could go!" I say. I'm practically vibrating from excitement.

Derrick looks around at his friends. "What makes you think you are the right one for such an important quest?" he says without looking at me.

I swim in front of Derrick so he *has* to look at me. "Because I'd do anything for my duck clan, and for my family," I breathe.

"What do you guys think?" says Derrick to the other ducks. He's still ignoring me.

"I don't know," says Donna. "It's a pretty important job for someone as weird-looking as Frank." Dexter and Dennis are nodding.

I swim up to Donna. "I know I can do it." Then I turn

and swim back to Derrick. "I know I can do it," I say again. "Please?"

"There might be a problem, though," says Derrick.

"Problem? What problem?" I say.

"The quester has to leave right away. Immediately. No goodbyes or anything. The health of the entire duck clan depends on you!"

"But," I say, "my mom will think something bad happened to me. She'll think I got eaten by the fox."

"Don't worry about that," says Derrick. "We'll tell her."

"Okay, I guess," I say. "Do you promise?"

"Hey, I'm your friend, remember?" Derrick puts a wing on my back for a moment. "Don't worry about a thing."

"But wait," I say. "I don't even know what I'm looking for."

"Oh yeah," says Derrick. "Um, what's Frank looking for out there, guys?"

"Well," says Donna, "an amulet?"

"Exactly," says Derrick. "We're going to need an amulet. An especially powerful amulet . . . for protection. We need to find a new, safe pond, and we'll need protection for the journey since not everyone can fly."

"So how . . . ?" I hesitate for a moment because I don't know very much about amulets yet. Are you supposed to know what to look for, or are you supposed to just find them by luck? I decide to ask. "How do I know what to look for?"

Derrick squints at me and moves in so close his beak almost touches mine. "Tooth, bone, and claw," he says. "From a predator!"

⚜ Chapter 7 ⚜

"From the mouth of death, from the enemy's paw," says Derrick. "Tooth, bone, and claw." He starts repeating himself. "From the mouth of death, from the enemy's paw . . ."

And then Donna, Dennis, and Dexter take it up and start chanting, "Tooth, bone, and claw. From the mouth of death, from the enemy's paw."

"Where . . . ? How am I going to . . . ?" But nobody's listening. And no one is going to answer my questions.

"Tooth, bone, and claw," they chant.

And since I can't think of anything else to do, I start chanting too. "Tooth, bone, and claw. From the mouth of death, from the enemy's paw." Chills run down my spine when I say these words. It would be so unusual and unexpected to find a tooth, bone, and claw. *From a predator!* That would have to be a powerful amulet.

And as we're chanting, I begin to see that we are all swimming, paddling to the shore. I am in the lead. I touch the land under my feet and stand up. As soon as I do, the chanting stops and Derrick steps in close again.

"Bring back tooth, bone, and claw from the skeleton of a predator," he says. "Not from some stupid grass-eater. Do not return without them!" He paddles back. "Now off on your quest! Hooray for Frank the Fearless!"

"Hooray for Frank the Fearless!" the others say.

My heart fills with pride, and I step out of the water. "I'm off!" I say.

"Don't come back without those amulets," says Derrick. "We're counting on you!" And then he and the other Fab Four ducks turn tail and swim away.

"Don't forget to tell my mom where I went!" I shout after them. But they don't turn around, so I don't know if they heard me.

I look into the forest beyond the grass around the pond. I've never been in the forest before. It looks dark. I don't even know if I'm allowed to go into the forest. My legs feel cold . . . and my legs never feel cold, even when I go swimming in the early morning pond.

But I have to do this. For the sake of the clan. I look back at the pond. I can't see the Fab Four anywhere. I want to go back and say goodbye to my mother and Darryl and Darlene. But what if Mother won't let me go? What if she says I'm too young? I could lose my chance to be a hero and make her proud. The more I think about it, the more I think she won't understand why I have to go.

I turn back and face the forest. Step by step, I tell myself. Just one step at a time, and keep an eye out for a tooth or a bone . . . or a claw.

I take a step and trip over a rock that is hiding in the grass. I fall flat on my beak. When I stand back up, I notice that it isn't a rock, because it is blinking at me.

"Oops," I say. "Sorry about . . . TR, is that you? Are you okay?"

"I didn't even feel anything," says TR.

I look around to see if anyone is watching me. No one is. "TR, I've been worried about you," I say. "Have you heard there's a fox prowling around here?"

"Foxes don't bother turtles," says TR.

"Well, they definitely bother ducks," I say. "By the way, you shouldn't be hiding in the grass waiting to trip someone up like that."

"I hope you're not going on that stupid quest," says TR.

"How do you even know anything about that?" I say. "And anyway, it isn't stupid. I might be able to save the pond."

"Bones and teeth and blah, blah, blah."

"Wow, turtles sure are good at minding someone else's business. And for your information, those are amulets, not blah, blah, blah. What do you know about anything?"

"I know that you shouldn't go into the forest alone. Actually you shouldn't go into the forest at all, but especially not alone."

"My friends say I could be a hero," I say.

"Those are not your friends," says TR.

"Hey, that's what my mom says," I say. "And it just shows how much you know, because both of you are wrong." I take two steps toward the forest. "And I'm going to show you how wrong you are."

I take two more steps, and I wish I wasn't alone. I wish Derrick and the others were coming with me. Something bumps into the back of my foot. It's TR.

"What are you doing?" I say.

"I'm coming with you," says TR.

"I thought you just said it was a stupid quest," I say.

"It *is* a stupid quest," says TR. "But no one should go into the forest alone, even if they are on a stupid quest."

I think about this. I hate that TR calls it a stupid quest, but part of me is really glad to not be alone.

"You can come with me on one condition," I say. TR doesn't say anything, so I continue. "The condition is that you don't call it a stupid quest anymore. Deal?"

TR blinks at me a few times. "Deal," she says finally. "But I'm going to think it the whole entire way."

We move toward the forest together.

❀❀❀ Chapter 8 ❀❀❀

At the edge of the tree line, I turn around to look back at my pond and consider what I'm about to do. The afternoon is starting to cool. A chilly breeze is stirring above the pond, but it feels great to be alive, especially if you're about to become a hero.

Things might have turned out terribly. I could have been born anything. When you're curled up in your shell, you have no idea what you are. You could be a slimy tadpole or a bug-eyed fish. You could be some scary reptile, snaking around on your belly your whole life. Or you could be a hardheaded turtle like TR. I turned out to be a bird with feathers and wings that will take me into the sky. And not just a bird, but a duck, the luckiest of all birds.

I look down. TR has followed and is looking up, waiting for me.

"Are you ready to do this?" I ask.

"Ready," she says. For sure I'm glad that I said she could come. For sure I don't want to be alone right now.

"Onward into the forest." I point my wing into the darkness. The earth has never felt so firm before. My feet tingle. I blink to clear the dizziness from my head. I have the strange feeling that if I tip sideways and fall over, I'll break into a thousand pieces.

A tumble of questions fill my mind and make me want to pause and think. I try to push on, but instead my feet stop walking.

TR steps ahead of me and I watch her progress, realizing this is the first time I've seen her walk on land. Her shell rolls back and forth and bumps and rocks with each step. She doesn't look like *her* feet are tingling. It also looks like turtles don't walk very fast.

I unstick my feet from where they seem to have put down roots. I can't back out now. This is my quest—and it isn't a good sign if you start your quest by not keeping up with a turtle. I hustle until I'm beside her.

It's a different kind of light under the trees. I feel strange, but when I look up I can see the sun straight overhead. That makes me feel better. Little birds fly quickly in between the trees and then disappear like they are in a big hurry.

I think of another reason to be glad. When you're in the egg, you don't know who your family is going to be. You could end up with a hard-shelled turtle for a mother who doesn't even know if you turned out to be a dud or not. Nobody wants that. Or worse, your family could be super popular—in a not-so-good way. Mom could have been a tender snail with a crispy shell and a chewy center that everyone thinks is delicious except me. Sometimes it's best not to be popular.

I have a mother who loves me in the best way. That thought makes a cloud form in my mind. I'm sad not to be saying goodbye to her, but I know she would never let me go. And she will be so delighted when I come back and save the duck pond.

I was the luckiest of all hatches. And now I am on an important quest.

We walk in silence for a while, which is hard for me. Finally I just have to say something.

"TR," I say, "remember to keep a lookout for bones."

"Bones, blah, blah, blah," she says, and then she mumbles something that might end with the word "stupid."

I decide to ignore it. "The sooner we find the bones and everything, the sooner we can go back home."

TR stops. "You think animals are just dying all the time and leaving their bones all over?" she says.

I stop. "I don't know," I say. "I never looked for bones before. But anyway, just . . ."

TR is moving again and shaking her head while she's walking. I think maybe I should change the subject.

"Hey, TR," I say.

She doesn't answer. I try to think of something new to talk about.

"Are you okay with the name I gave you?"

"I'm thinking about it." She doesn't turn her head, but I know she can tell I'm right here.

After that I can't think of anything else to say. We walk in silence. Step after step. I think about how far we are getting from the pond . . . and home. Now I can't see the sun no matter how I look up or twist my neck around. And then the air turns cold, and the trees stop looking so much like trees and start looking more like shapes. I should have waited until morning to begin my quest.

The light gets steadily dimmer until I can't really see the ground, which my toes find out when I trip over a rock. I pick myself up.

TR just bumps her way into the gloom of the shapes.

"Can you see okay?" My voice sounds way too loud in this place.

"Mmm." TR doesn't stop or turn her head.

"What does 'Mmm' mean?" I whisper. It's getting darker. "Can you see or not?" I can only see a few shadows and blobs around us, and it bothers me quite a bit. Not that I'm going to admit it. But any number of dangers could be waiting behind that tall blob right ahead. Or that one to the side. The blobs get bigger as we walk too, which could mean the dangers are getting bigger.

TR keeps walking.

I lean down. "Well?" I whisper into her earhole.

TR turns. "Well what?"

Whispering makes me even more afraid, so I go back to talking in a normal voice. "Can you see or not? And what does 'Mmm' mean when I ask you a question?"

"I can't see a thing," TR says slowly. "But that doesn't mean much because turtles can't see very well anyway."

I look to one side and then the other and then behind because I have a sudden feeling something might be sneaking up on me. Seeing nothing doesn't put my mind at ease at all. "So why do you keep walking if you can't see where you're going?"

"I thought we were on a quest," TR says. "I thought we were going somewhere. And pardon me for saying this, but turtles have this crazy idea that to get somewhere, you have to keep moving."

"Someone is watching us," I say. I whip around in a circle.

"No one is watching us." TR keeps going straight ahead.

"Oh yeah?" I practice my surprisingly strong duck bites in the air around my head. "Then why are my tail feathers tingling?"

"I don't know, parasites?" TR looks back at me. "Is it kind of an itching tingling? I've heard birds can get a lice thing right there at the base of the tail that itches like the dickens."

"I don't have lice!" I shout. I listen to my voice bounce off the trees, which makes the tingling in my tail worse.

"I don't have lice," I whisper. "But I do have a feeling that someone is watching us." I turn in a circle again, and again I see nothing.

TR doesn't answer, so I decide to continue walking and keep up with her.

The light fades further. Dark blobs between the trees turn out to be . . . spaces . . . between the trees. Just spaces, I tell myself, not duck-eating blobs. But I'm still glad I'm not alone. Which, when I think about it, gives me a weird feeling.

I mean, is TR really a friend? Can ducks and turtles be friends? Probably not. Ducks are fliers, turtles are crawlers. Ducks are soft, turtles are hard. Ducks are nice to look at, and . . . I know it isn't nice to say this, but turtles are ugly. Ducks and turtles are just too different. There is no way TR and I can actually be friends, because ducks are naturally suspicious and I'm a good duck.

We walk and walk until I'm sure I've never walked this far in my whole life, and then we walk some more, and I notice that a forest gets gloomy as night comes. Which means the dark blobs get darker, and they seem more and more like duck-eating blobs.

"Let's find a place to hole up for the night," I say.

I kick dust and pine needles toward an extra-dark blob. It turns out to be a hole at the base of a tree, which is what I was hoping for. Carefully, I stretch one foot into the hole.

I wiggle my toes around. Yep. It's a hole. Dry inside. I put my head down and listen. Most important, there is no one living there who wants to bite a duck head.

I hop in. I hear TR pull herself in behind me and settle down.

As soon as she's still, I scooch closer.

Oof. Snuggling with a turtle is no good at all. I shift to try to get more comfortable. It doesn't help. I scoot my body to the side and put my head on her back. Hard as a rock.

"TR?" I whisper.

She doesn't answer. She's probably sleeping . . . or she knows I'm going to ask a question, and sometimes it seems like she hates my questions.

I lie with my head on her shell and refuse to close my eyes. Not that I can see anything. In fact, I try something out. I close my eyes and then open them and then close them again and then open them. It's exactly the same.

But something is bothering me, and it's not just that my head is on a pillow as hard as a river rock.

It's the noises . . . or rather, the not-noises. I've spent every night of my life with pond noises in my ears, like the sound of the stream, croaking frogs, and every once in a while a splash from a jumping fish. But the forest is silent.

Except it isn't. I start hearing sounds I didn't notice before.

I pick my head up.

Noises seem to be coming from all around the tree.

And the harder I listen, the more I think the worst noise is coming from inside the hole. It's a horrible scratching sound.

My tail feathers tingle even more than before. I rap my beak on TR's shell. "TR," I hiss. "Wake up."

"Huh?" she says.

"Listen," I say. I wait for her to hear it too. But the scratching noise has stopped. I try to quiet the pounding of my heart. "I heard something. Something bad. Like . . . something that wants to eat us."

"What did it sound like?" TR asks.

"It was a really, really scary scratching sound," I say. "And it sounded like it was right here in the hole with us."

TR doesn't say anything for a while. I listen with all my feathers quivering. Finally she says, "Did it sound like this?"

I hear the same scratching sound. It fills the hole again, but it's coming from under TR. It doesn't sound so scary anymore. "Is that you?" I whisper.

"Yes."

"Why are you making that I'm-going-to-sneak-up-on-you-and-eat-you scratching sound?"

"Sneakers are quiet. That's how they sneak," says TR.

I think about this. She has a point. "Well, then why

were you making that I'm-going-to-dig-you-out-and-eat-you-alive scratching sound?"

"I was making a little sleep hole for myself."

"Oh." I turn to get comfortable and lean against her shell again. "Well, don't. Some of us are trying to sleep. No more scratching . . . or digging, or whatever."

I lie there thinking about how ducks tuck their heads under their wings. How ducks murmur little duck noises. How satisfying duck habits are for going to sleep. And how much I'm going to enjoy being back in the duck pond when my quest is finished.

Chapter 9

The next thing I know, I'm awake and it's light and I'm alone. I scramble out of the dusty hole and see pine trees all around me. The trees are different from the ones near the pond.

"TR?" I call. Did I upset her the night before? Did she decide to turn around and go back to the pond? She doesn't move all that fast, so maybe she can still hear me. "I'm sorry!" I shout. "You can scratch a little sleep hole next time if you want."

Something rustles on the other side of a bush.

"Or a *big* sleep hole!" I shout.

Something rustles a little louder.

I walk slowly toward the sound and see a grassy patch and TR in the middle of it with grass sticking out the sides of her mouth.

"You left me." I give her a glare.

She shakes her head and blinks.

"Yes you did," I say. "I thought I might have to make this quest alone. All by myself."

The grass at the sides of her mouth moves up and down with each chew. Then a truly ugly gray tongue comes out and pulls in more grass. TR chews a little longer, blinks again, and then swallows. "Hungry," she says finally.

"Well, you still could have woken me up before you snuck out." I clip a tall piece of grass with my beak. It's sweet and I look around for more. "Why didn't you answer me when I called?" I take another bite of grass.

"My mouth was full." TR tears off some more grass and chews.

"Did you see any bones while you were looking for breakfast?" I say.

TR doesn't stop chewing, but she lowers her eyelids halfway to show me what she thinks of my question. Greenish foam squeezes out of the corners of her mouth. Her gray tongue moves slowly, squishing the foam. I've never seen a turtle eat before, and now I wish I never had. I want to look away, but I can't.

"You're gross," I say.

Finally the last bit of grass disappears and TR gulps. "You're grumpy."

"I like grass too, you know." I act like it's nothing to say what I'm saying. But I'm nervous that she'll think I'm weird, just like everyone else does.

She swallows again. "So?"

"You probably thought ducks ate snails and bugs," I say. "Well, I like the taste of grass. Is that such a bad thing? Can't someone be a little different now and then?"

She shakes her head. "You're still grumpy."

"Well, I deserve to be grumpy," I say. "I'm starting my bad mood early." I spin around on one webbed foot. "Let's go."

We walk and walk. In fact, we walk all morning over hills and then back down to cool streams. The cool streams are what I look forward to. I eat the grass at the sides of the streams, but my favorite thing to do is find a deep part, even if it is a tiny pool only big enough for me to paddle around in.

And we walk all afternoon. I go under some logs that are lying on the ground, and over other logs. TR can only go under. Before the sun disappears, we try to find a not-scary place to spend the night.

The next morning we start out again.

"Don't forget to look for bones," I say.

"I don't care about bones," says TR. "Looking for bones is stupid."

"Hey," I say. "You promised not to call my quest stupid."

"I didn't say anything about your quest," says TR. "I just said looking for bones is stupid."

Late in the afternoon, when we get to a stream, TR says, "Look over there."

"Where?" I say. I'm not really looking because I'm too busy feeling wonderful, letting the water flow over my toes even though this stream is too shallow for swimming.

"Over there," she says.

Poor TR doesn't have any wings or even a beak for pointing, so it would be pretty hard to see what she's talking about even if I wasn't concentrating on the cool water.

"Looks like a bone to me," she says.

"Where?" Now I'm paying attention, and I jump out of the stream. I run over to the thing TR is looking at, and I walk around it. I'm pretty sure it's a bone, and I am so excited.

TR walks over slowly.

"I'm almost positive it's a bone," I say. "It's white and skinny and . . ."

"And bony," says TR.

"Yes," I say, "it's very bony."

"And big," says TR.

I take a step back. TR is right . . . as usual. This bone is huge.

"Maybe we can break a piece of it off," I say. I pick up the bone in my beak, but it is so heavy I can barely walk with it, even with one end dragging on the ground. I pull it over to a rock and let it fall.

It clunks softly against the rock and doesn't break. I do this two more times. Nothing. I try to lift it a fourth time, but I'm too tired and I let it go. I'm so disappointed.

"It isn't a predator bone anyhow," says TR.

"What?" I say. "How do you know?"

"Too big," says TR. "Predators are small and quick."

"Why didn't you say something when I was trying to break it on the rock?" I say.

"You said you wanted me to keep a lookout for bones, so I did."

"Thanks a lot. Next time just tell me if you see some predator bones."

We start walking again. I'm really grouchy. I'm so grouchy I'm pretty certain nothing could cheer me up.

"Hey, Frank!" shouts TR.

She's a long way behind me because when I get grouchy I like to walk faster and be alone.

"What?" I shout back without turning around.

"Are those feathers I see sprouting up out of your wings?" she shouts.

I turn around in a hurry. Is it true? It is! I check out the rest of me while TR catches up. I'm starting to grow back feathers too. And also . . . I'm pretty sure I can just see some chest feathers poking through.

"Won't be long now before you'll be a flier," says TR. "Those feathers will start to come in real fast."

My heart feels so light and happy that I wonder if I could take flight right this moment! Of course, when I flap my wings to try, nothing happens. No flight feathers yet. But I practically dance my way to the end of the day.

The next morning begins warm. Too warm. When the sun is high in the sky, the air that should be cool and shady under the trees is hot and sticky. My wide, webbed feet, so excellent for swimming, are not so great for walking through bushes, under branches, over stumps and logs, up and down hills. Behind me, I hear the *swish, bump, swish, bump* as TR drags her shell step by step.

For a while, I walk ahead, scoping out the best trails where a four-legger with a house on her back won't get stuck. Then I slow down to show her the way or stop and wait for her to catch up.

I miss the sound of ducks talking loudly all the time. Here, all I can hear is a turtle walking and the buzzing of bugs. A great cloud of tiny insects buzzes around me. Every time I shake my head, they buzz louder. I snap my beak at them. To my surprise, I catch four or five of the little pests. They taste just as bad as I remember.

TR is not a fast walker. Not as fast as a duck. Ducks walk . . . duckly. Which is a lot faster than a turtle. Sometimes I stand still and let her pass me. All she does is nod because apparently turtles don't talk very much. One thing about her, though, is that she doesn't seem to get tired, and she doesn't give up. One time, I see she's dragging a stick that got stuck on the underside of her shell.

"Hey, TR," I say.

She doesn't seem to hear.

I stand on the stick to get it unstuck. Instead it drags me along the ground, scraping a little trail in the pine needles for a few paces. But finally it comes loose. TR doesn't stop or even seem to notice.

"How do we know we're going the right way?" I hop off the stick and step along after TR.

"We don't," says TR. "Bones and teeth, blah, blah, blah. We gotta find them. Isn't that what your so-called friends told you?" She doesn't turn her head.

"Friends. Not so-called friends," I say.

TR answers but I don't hear what she says. I'm not really listening because I hear a strange sound. So far we haven't seen another forest creature, unless bugs and small birds count.

"Frank!" TR whispers. "This way."

I look at her. TR clearly can hear better than she can see. She's moving in the opposite direction from the sound.

I tip my head to listen better. What makes that kind of sound? I ignore TR's advice and flap-step around a bush to see. Something is scrabbling, which, by my guess, shouldn't be too dangerous for a duck. Maybe it is a squirrel. Acorns are hunted by scrabblers. Ducks are hunted by sneaky and quiet animals.

✴️ Chapter 10 ✴️

I see a long bare tail. No feathers. No fur. No hair on this tail.

The tail is connected to a dull white creature looking up into a small tree.

Ugh.

This creature is the very opposite of a beautiful duck. It has round ears sticking out of a mean-looking pointed face, and the ears are as naked as its tail. "TR," I whisper as softly as I can.

I wish I'd listened to her. I wish I'd gone the other direction. The sight of this animal makes me shiver. I start to back up—too late.

The thing turns its skinny head and smiles at me, uncovering a long row of sharp gray teeth, the same color as the hair on its face. Should I run? Should I act like I'm not staring? Should I just stand here?

"Hello," the thing says in a raspy voice.

"Frank." I look down and see TR is bumping my leg. "It's a possum. Let's get out of here."

I want to go. Instead, for some reason, I say, "Hello."

"Hey, dummy." TR bumps my leg again. "Possums eat birds."

The thing is still staring at me. Its short legs don't seem like they can run very fast. But something about this fellow makes me suspicious.

"What are you searching for in that tree?" I ask.

The possum looks slowly up the tree and then back at me. "That's neither here nor there."

Why am I standing here talking to a thing with a tail like that and teeth like those? It's as if my feet are stuck to the forest floor. The possum turns his attention back up the tree. I try to see what he is so interested in.

Then I find it. A nest on a low branch. Not very high at all. I know what's inside a nest. Eggs. Helpless little chicks thinking how great it will be to finally hatch.

"Are you hunting?" I say. "Are you hunting bird babies that are so small and defenseless they can't fight back or even run away?"

The possum grabs the tree with both front paws and gazes up at the nest. "It's true they are a bit small," he rasps. "But ever so tasty." Then he looks back at me. "And their little bird bones have a satisfying crunch." He begins to climb the tree as easily as if he were walking on land. Then he reaches a paw up and into the nest. A small light blue egg appears at the lip of the nest and teeters for a moment.

My breath catches in my throat.

The egg drops.

"Oops," says the possum.

There's a sickening crack, and I stare as clear and yellow ooze makes a tiny puddle on the pine needles under the broken shell.

"Murderer!" I shout.

"Don't worry, there's more." The possum's paw is already back in the nest, reaching for a second egg. Without thinking, I fling myself over the ground, jump and flap into the air, grab the hairless tail in my beak, and pull.

I can feel the possum slip a bit. Then his claws hold fast to the tree.

"Mmm, mmm, mmm." I can't speak. But I can pull. I pull hard and flap my wings. I begin to swing.

Suddenly the possum's heavy body is hurtling toward me. I hit the ground, and the possum hits the ground next to me with a thud. I hop to my feet and find myself beak-to-nose with a pointy, drippy, toothy snout.

"You sh-sh-sh-sh-shouldn't have done that." The possum lifts his lips to show more teeth. It isn't a smile. "Nobody pullsssssssss my tail," he hisses. "Nobody *ever* grabs my tail and pullssssss me out of a tree."

"Well, you . . . you . . ." I back up. The possum matches me step for step. "You shouldn't . . . Those babies were defenseless."

"Defensssssssssseless, yessssssssss." Bubbles of spit fly out between the rows of teeth. "But not you. Sssssssso, defend yourself."

The possum opens his mouth. I see spikes. I try to back up some more, but I run into a tree behind me. I squeeze my eyes shut and squawk. I hear a snap of teeth.

Nothing. No pain. No crunching neck bones. I'm still alive!

Wow! I had no idea I had such a ferocious squawk. I scared that possum right off. What a weapon! I open my eyes to look at my frightened predator.

The possum is not looking at me. He is looking at his tail. And on the end of that tail is a brown bump.

"TR!" I shout. "What are you doing?"

TR doesn't answer. Her turtle jaws are clamped on the possum's tail, and her head is pulled as far as possible into her shell. Her feet are all tucked up inside her shell too, and her eyes are closed.

My brain freezes. I can't think what to do.

The possum reaches around and scratches at TR's scaly head and then at her shell with his long claws. He tries to chew her shell. "Nobody!" *Scratch, scratch, chew, chew.* "Pulls!" *Scratch, bite.* "On my tail!" He stops biting and scratching and stumbles off, dragging TR behind him.

My brain unfreezes. I run alongside TR. "Let go!"

I shout. "TR, you can let go now!" I can't tell if she can hear me. Suddenly her shell goes over a root and lurches sideways, slamming into me. From the dirt where I fall, I yell one more time. "TR, let go now!"

But TR hangs on, bumping along behind, sometimes rolling over, but not letting go and not sticking her legs out. The possum stops to scratch at TR's shell one more time and hisses before starting to run again. They disappear behind a stand of trees. For a short while I can hear the thumping of a turtle shell along the ground. Then silence.

I jump up and run after TR and the possum, but they've gone out of sight. Should I follow? I'm worried about my friend, but I'm also worried about the eggs that the possum wanted to eat. I hope TR lets go very soon.

I hurry back to the tree, where the small nest is still perched on the lowest branch. On the ground, resting against a root, is the first broken egg. There is a second egg nearby that must have rolled out after I grabbed the possum's tail. I check on it. It looks okay. Maybe it can still be saved. It's blue with little darker blue spots. But then I see a jagged crack through the middle. I reach out my webbed toes gently to touch it.

Suddenly the forest air splits open with a scream so loud I can't tell where it's coming from. Instinctively, I duck. A flurry of wingbeats and a painful pounding from a sharp beak rains down on me.

I cover my head with my wings as I run.

The attacker bombs me again and again from above, finding spaces between my wings to score hit after hit.

"Stop," I quack.

"Beast! Monster! Fiend!" screams my attacker.

I trip on a tree root and fall flat on my beak.

"Baby killer!" My attacker gets in another bull's-eye on my noggin.

Baby killer? I jump up and start running again. I can't weave or bob my head fast enough to get away, but now I think I understand. It's the poor mother of those eggs. I dash under a low-growing tree, where the branches will protect me, and spin around. "Hey!" I shout. "Do I look like an egg-eater?"

The mother bird flutters in front of my face so fast I can't see her wings. Then she comes to rest on a branch above my head. Her blue wings twitch like she might be thinking of attacking again. She looks down at me.

"Ouch," I say, rubbing my head. "I'm really sorry about your babies, but please stop trying to peck my brain out. It wasn't me."

The bird hops sideways. She checks me up and down. I can see why my head is so sore. Even though she's not very big, her beak is sharp and dangerous-looking. She has a dark band across her eyes.

I get ready to run again if she attacks. Instead she lets out a sad cry.

I duck and climb out from under the branches. "It wasn't me," I say one more time, and rub the top of my crown.

But when I look up, she's gone.

⚛ Chapter 11 ⚛

"**H**ey, TR!" I stumble back the way I came. "Where are you?" I yell. I retrace my steps the best I can, and pretty soon I can follow the trail of a possum dragging a turtle through the trees. It isn't very hard because the heavy shell attached to a surprisingly strong set of turtle teeth—or whatever turtles have—leaves a wide track on the ground where the pine needles have been pushed aside.

Why didn't TR let go? Is she okay? That is one stubborn turtle. And probably mad, which makes me want to be her friend even more.

The trail leads down a slope. At the bottom is a stream, and the trail goes right into the stream. Did that possum think he could make my turtle friend let go by drowning her? Ha! TR was born for the water. But now I have a problem. There is no more trail to follow. I look to the other side of the stream—the trail does not start up again.

I decide to call some more. "Hey, TR . . ." Then I stop. What if the possum *did* shake TR off his tail? If that happened, he could follow my voice and come find me and chew me up.

But then I think of TR and what a good friend she is. I'm not going to stop calling for her just because I'm a little nervous about a mean old possum.

"TR!" I shout as loudly as I can. "Where are you?"

I listen for an answer, but I only hear the stream.

I walk downstream for a while, calling. And then I walk upstream. I remember that TR didn't answer one other time because she had her mouth full of grass. But she wouldn't be eating now, I think. Maybe she still has her mouth full of possum tail.

I go back to the turtle shell trail and I sit down and wait. Pretty soon my head is surrounded by a cloud of buzzing mosquitoes. They are all looking for a place to drink my blood. I shake my head when the air gets too buzzy, and I only get a moment's peace before they come back.

Then all at once they're gone.

I look around, wondering what just happened. I look up. The sun has disappeared and the sky is getting dark. There is a hum in the air all around my head. Suddenly the world is lit up by a terrible white light. The lightning has barely faded when the thunder cracks. It feels as if my brain has been grabbed by a giant possum and slammed against the side of my skull.

I fall to the ground, and then I get up and run in circles. The sound of thunder is still hot in my brain. "Mommy!" I scream, and I strike out running in a straight line. But no matter how far I run, I can't get away from the ringing in my head.

Suddenly a river of rain falls out of the sky. "Ahhh, rain!" I scream.

Then I stop. Rain? I'm a duck and I'm running away from rain? I look for a place to wait out the storm. I slip under a bush to rest and watch the downpour.

I snap awake when there is no more light left in the sky. I hadn't meant to fall asleep. The trees are dripping, but the rain has stopped. The ringing in my ears is gone, and quiet has never sounded so nice.

In the middle of the night, something wakes me up again. It's drizzling now, but that's not what woke me up. Voices. It sounds like they are right outside the leafy cover of my bush.

"But I'm hungry," says a whiny voice.

"Of course you're hungry," says another, lower voice. "Everyone's hungry. That's why we're out here hunting and wet in this lousy weather instead of staying dry and warm in our hole."

Hunters? I'm wide awake now.

"We're never going to catch anything anyway," says the first voice. "We never catch anything. Ever since we decided to be partners, we've had nothing but bad luck. It was a dumb idea. Stoats are supposed to be loners, not partners."

Stoats? I think I remember Mother mentioning stoats. And if they're hunting, they must be predators. I shiver.

"It was your dumb idea, Stumpy, in case you don't remember," says the second voice. "And now you don't even like your own dumb idea, so that makes you doubly dumb. 'I don't want to be lonely,' you said. But you talk too much, so we never catch anything. And now here we are with our empty stomachs in the wet and cold, hunting together and finding nothing. I can't smell a thing in this rain."

"Me neither," says the one called Stumpy. "Let's just go back to our hole and get dry, Boss. Everything just smells like wet bird out here."

"Hang on," says the one called Boss, and he drops his voice to a whisper. "You're right. It does smell like wet bird around here." The voices seem like they are just outside the bush I'm hiding under. My legs start trembling from fear.

"But Boss, I'm cold," says Stumpy.

"Quiet!" hisses Boss. "There's something here. Now, just watch the boss at work. We'll be crunching bones by sunrise."

I don't like this talk of bone crunching. I think about running, but I can't see anything in the darkness. And I don't know if a duck can outrun a stoat. There is a moment of silence, and then I hear a nose sniffing.

"I smell something," says Boss.

"A good something?" Stumpy wants to know.

"Very good."

"Then it must be me!" Stumpy laughs at his own joke in a high voice. "Hee, hee, hee."

"You? You smell like three-day-old garbage. Anyway, shut up, bonehead. You'll scare off the prey."

"Who are you calling garbage?"

"I'm calling garbage the only one here with a big mouth and breath like moldy cheese, garbage."

"Forget hunting. I'm going to teach you a lesson."

In the next instant, there is a big scuffling sound, and then two balls of fur come smashing in under my bush and almost crush me. Luckily no one seems to notice that a duckling is getting away.

I tiptoe out of my bush. Once I'm out in the open, I run. I can't see a thing in the dark, and before I've taken five steps I bump into a tree. But that doesn't stop me. I just keep running anyway.

Finally, when my legs can't keep moving, I pause and listen. The forest is quiet. The drizzle has stopped, and through the trees there is a glow that tells me it's almost morning.

I make myself small and listen for any scary stoat sounds.

When it gets light enough to really see, I look around. Nothing is familiar. I'm lost and I need a friend more than I ever did before. I open my beak to call for TR, but only a little squeak comes out. In my heart I know that it is no use hoping she can hear me. She is long gone.

Now, which way to go? I shake my head to try to clear the lost and sad feelings. I need to think.

It might be time to turn to my instincts. If only I knew what an instinct felt like. Just then something donks me on the head. I blink. I look up. Nothing but an old tree. I look down. A little dead stick.

But it must be a sign. An instinct sign. So I start walking in the direction I was facing when I got donked by the stick.

Nothing, not even stoats or possums or losing my best friend, will keep me from completing my quest. I keep a sharp eye out for bones.

✦ Chapter 12 ✦

It isn't the same to walk through a giant forest alone when you're used to walking with a friend. The trees look bigger, your footsteps sound louder, and you feel like you're being followed by some nasty predator. Actually, that part feels exactly the same.

I stop and look behind me often. I ask myself why I am here. To find the amulets, of course. But how do the amulets work? A bone or a tooth isn't like Mother's lucky stone with three dots.

Maybe I'll figure it out later. But thinking of Mother makes me lonelier. I wonder if Derrick and my other friends really told her where I went. Suddenly I don't want to be in the middle of all these tall, dark trees. I want to be back on my lovely clear pond, messing around with Darryl and Darlene, or just quietly watching the sun come up. Instead I'm waiting to be grabbed by the neck and slung over some evil duck-eater's back and fed to his nasty little duck-eater babies.

Then I remember my mother's face and her laugh, and I imagine her looking at me with delighted eyes, and I push on. I would walk a thousand days if I knew at the end of it I could make my mother proud.

I cross a mountain of rocks, I find my way through a thicket of thorns without getting too much duck fuzz ripped out, and I finally cool my feet in a forest stream.

I ignore the soft, secret noises behind me that are made by the footsteps of a sharp-toothed predator. They are all in my head, I tell myself. That breaking twig back there? It's my imagination. The whispers and scuffling in the leaves? Fantasy. The quiet, high-pitched giggling coming from behind the tree trunks? Nothing but my mind playing tricks on me.

"Did you hear that, TR?" It makes me feel better to talk to my friend even if she isn't beside me to hear it. "I'm going to turn around quickly just to prove that nothing is following me. And when I do, I'm going to laugh at myself and my crazy brain for scaring me over and over." One, two, three, look!

I blink.

"See that?" I say out loud. "I told you it was nothing but a couple of predators scurrying behind a tree."

Predators? Stoats?

Smaller than me, slinky and quick. My pulse starts thumping inside my head, and a tingling runs from my neck down my back.

I flap across the stream and stumble on some stones.

I get myself onto the other side and into some grass that might be good for hiding. I can hardly breathe, and the pounding in my head has not gone away. I try to calm myself and think.

I peek out of the grass. They aren't even pretending to hide any longer. They shout, "Whee!" and come romping and swimming across the stream toward me. They are light-brown-colored, with long tails and dark eyes, and *very* fast!

I ditch my grass cover and run. It would be so much better if I could only breathe. I can't feel my legs.

I break out into a little clearing. This would be a very good time to know how to fly. I flap my wings. It feels like it helps me run faster—I even sort of skim for a few seconds—but it definitely isn't the same as flying. And it is very tiring.

"Hee, hee, hee!" The stoats are having a wonderful time, and by the sound of their squeaky laughter, they are getting closer. I can hear the patter of little feet behind me, and I can almost feel claws around my neck. I turn to glance back while I run. They are streaking through the grass with their eyes locked on me.

Something grabs one of my legs, and I fall—*splat!*—beak first into the forest floor. The grabber lets go. I scramble up. The two stoats are dancing in a circle around me now.

"Hee, hee! Lookee here, Boss," says one. "A birdie!"

There is no place to run. I just stand there getting dizzy.

"What do you suppose is under those feathers, Stumpy?" says Boss.

"Something soft," says Stumpy.

"Something warm," says Boss.

"Soft and warm and juicy!" says Stumpy. "Whee!"

Just when I think I'm going to fall over from dizziness, they stop dancing around. A nose comes sniffing right up to my face. *Sniff, sniff, sniff.* The stoat has a big sharp-toothed grin. I take a step back and bump into something furry.

"Where are you going, Birdie?" says Boss. I turn around.

"Want me to do 'im, Boss?" says the stoat behind me. "Want me to give the neck bite? Huh? A bite right through the neck?"

"Just hold on, harebrain," says Boss. He is in my face, and his breath smells rotten. "No hurry. Do we want to drag Birdie to our den or do we want him to walk there on his own two feet?"

"Um . . . drag 'im?"

"No, stupid. We like our food clean, remember? When you drag your food it gets dirty. Make him walk. But if he runs . . ." Boss stands up on his hind feet and stares into my eyes. "Then, Stumpy, take him out with one bite."

"Hee, hee," says Stumpy. "I hope he runs!"

"March, birdbrain," says Boss. "And if you run . . . if we have to chase you down again . . . one bite from my associate here and you'll have taken your last step." He opens both front paws so I can see his very sharp claws.

I try to force my heart rate down. "Where are you taking me?" I ask. My voice trembles.

"None of your beeswax," says Boss. "And no more questions."

"Yeah," says Stumpy. "None of your beeswax." He gives me a push. "Hey, Boss. If he asks a question, that's the same as running, right? I get to bite him, right?"

"Right," says Boss. "No questions and no running. Now go."

We start moving. Boss goes in front, and I watch his hunched-up way of walking and wonder why I thought a journey through a forest was such a good idea. I wonder if Derrick and the other ducks in the Fab Four gang knew that this quest was going to be so dangerous. My legs feel wobbly. Stumpy steps in behind and to the side of me. He walks low to the ground on his short legs.

"So I guess you're taking me to your hole," I say. I have to be careful not to ask any questions.

"Yep," says Stumpy.

"It's not a hole. It's a den," says Boss.

"Yeah, it's a den," says Stumpy. "So don't call it a hole."

I decide I really hate stoats. They are going to kill and eat me, and they are making me walk so they don't have to drag my dead body. That makes me mad. Which is better than feeling scared.

"I bet your hole is dirty," I say. And I notice that my voice isn't trembling like before.

"It's not dirty," says Boss. "We don't like dirt, so we cleaned it out."

"Yeah," says Stumpy. "We cleaned it out because we like things to be clean."

"I bet it still has dirt in it," I say. My feet keep moving, but now I start looking for a place to run. I think about how my wings helped me while I was running and how I could make myself skim above the ground for a few steps. If I can find a downhill, I might be able to use my wings to go faster than these fur faces.

"I guess it does still have dirt in it," says Stumpy after a few minutes. "Hey, Boss, does it still have dirt in it?"

"Of course it has dirt in it," says Boss. "It's a hole in the ground."

"I told you it's a hole," I say.

Boss stops and turns around. "Hey, smart mouth. It *was* a hole. But we cleaned it out, so now it is a den, okay?" He starts walking again, up the side of a hill.

"I bet Boss found it," I say. "Dirt for a floor, dirt for a

ceiling, and dirt for walls. It sounds dirty."

"It's a little dirty," says Stumpy.

"I thought you like it clean," I say.

"It's not dirty. It's cozy," says Boss.

"Yeah, it's cozy," says Stumpy. "And don't say nothing different."

"I know what the best thing is to put in a hole," I say.

"What?" says Stumpy.

"Dirt," I say. "Dirt and garbage is the best thing to put in a dirt hole."

"Stumpy!" Boss walks faster. "Stop talking to this bird. He's making me mad."

"Want me to bite him, Boss?" says Stumpy.

"No, you bonehead." Boss stops, reaches over me with a front paw, and whacks Stumpy on the noggin.

"Ouch!" says Stumpy.

"Now shut your yap," says Boss. "We need the bird to walk. We're almost to our hole . . . I mean our *den* . . . and we don't want our food to get dirty."

We walk a few more steps uphill, and then Boss stops and I see we're standing at the opening to a hole that goes down into the hillside. I look around and notice that we are at the top of the slope we just walked up.

My heart thumps in my chest. If I can just get these two distracted, I might be able to make a run for it.

"Stumpy, are you ready to eat?" says Boss. "This is the

moment you were waiting for. Go ahead and bite his neck."

"Hold it," I say. "I thought you said you had a clean home. I think I see some dirt."

"Where?" says Stumpy.

I take a step closer to the den, and I push a little pile of sticks and pine needles into it, trying—but not too hard—to make it look like an accident.

"Hey," says Boss. "Stop that."

"Oops," I say. "Sorry about that."

"Stumpy," Boss growls, "this bird is really gonna get it. But first, GET THAT DIRT OUT OF OUR DEN!"

"Sure, Boss." Stumpy pokes his head down the hole and starts to scoop out the pine needles.

This is my chance. "Oh my gosh!" I scream. "Watch out, everyone. It's a fox!"

Stumpy bumps his head on the ceiling of the hole. From the corner of my eye I see Boss whirl around, looking for the fox. I race downhill as fast as I can.

"Hey, Stumpy!" shouts Boss. "He's getting away. Come on!"

"What about the fox?" calls Stumpy.

I spread my wings. My feet are racing as much as duck feet can race.

"It's a trick!" yells Boss. "Come on!"

I can feel him right behind me. I flap my wings. *Flap, flap, flap.* My legs lift off the ground. I'm flying! Well, not flying exactly. More like skimming. Up ahead the downhill is coming to an end. At the bottom is a clump of grass, and I'm heading right for it. There is no way for me to slow down. I plow into the grass. *Whoosh!*

I scramble up. There is no more downhill, so I start running back up the other side. My wings can't help me now, and my legs are getting tired.

I don't even hear Boss come up behind me. I don't smell his breath or feel his paws. Instead I get knocked off my feet and slammed into the ground. My breath whomps out of me.

We roll back down to the bottom of the hill, and I can feel Boss's paws clamped around my neck.

We stop. No escape. I can hardly breathe. I want to scream out for Mom even though I know I'm far, far away from her. "Mommy!" My voice comes out even quieter than a whisper because I can't catch my breath.

"Stumpy, you better get down here in a hurry!" Boss yells right into my ear. "I know you wanted to bite him first, but if you don't get here fast, I'm going to do it myself."

I hear Boss's voice as if it is coming from the other end of a hollow log. I'm not trembling any longer. I just want to see my family again. I want to be in my nest. And I want to feel Mom's wing over my back.

"Wait! Wait!" I can hear Stumpy scrambling down the hill. "Let me do it. I want to bite his neck."

Boss picks me up and puts me on my feet. His paws are still around my neck. I can hardly stand. I feel dizzy.

"I'll hold him, and you bite," says Boss.

Stumpy runs toward us. "I'm ready!" He clicks his sharp teeth together.

Boss stretches my neck out. I close my eyes.

Suddenly I hear the most awful noise, one that I might have heard once before. It is a screeching and a wailing that splits the air, louder and louder, and ends with a crack.

❧ Chapter 13 ❧

I get thrown to the ground. Stoat paws trample my legs, my back, my head.

"Get it off me!" screams Stumpy.

The shrieking doesn't stop.

Rap, rap, rap.

Suddenly there are no stoats on top of me. No long toes around my neck. I roll over, sit up, and shake my head to see what Stumpy is screaming about. He is spinning in a circle. I have to blink twice to be sure, but there is a bird over Stumpy's head, and it's swooping in, hammering away on the top of his skull with its beak. Stumpy is grabbing at it and shaking his head, but this bird is really quick. "Help! Help!"

"Stop turning and let me grab it." Boss is reaching up with his paws.

The bird stops pounding the top of Stumpy's crown. It has a dark stripe across its eyes, and its beak is small but sharp. Instinctively I protect my head. I think I know this bird!

In a flash the bird attacks Boss's head. *Rap, rap.* The bird darts in with a perfect strike, then flies out of reach from the stoat's claws, circles around, and dives in again.

"Ow, ow, ow!" Now it is Boss's turn to spin in a circle. "Get this thing away from me! Help!"

But Stumpy isn't feeling very helpful. He is churning back up the hill toward his den in a cloud of dust.

I back up a few steps. Part of me wants to run away as fast as I can in case I'm next. But another part just wants to watch.

Boss spins and spins, which works. But as soon as he stops, the bird attacks again. Boss shakes his head. The bird's beak just keeps pounding on the top of that thick stoat skull. And the screeching doesn't stop either. It sounds almost like crying but loud. Very loud.

Finally, Boss does like Stumpy and tears uphill toward his hole. The bird follows about halfway and gets in about four extra whacks before it flies off. Boss doesn't stop running until he gets to his den, where he dives in headfirst.

When I can't see any more stoats, I shake my head to clear it. What just happened? I look up and see that the attack bird has come back and is on a branch just above me. It's looking right at me as if it might attack again. I give a little quack and back up.

But instead of attacking, the bird makes a sad little sound. I know where I've seen it . . . I mean *her* . . . before. I just don't know why she's here. This is the same bird who thought I killed her babies. Last time we met, it was me that was getting pounded instead of a couple of stoats. She shakes her head, and stoat hairs float quietly away in the air.

I take a step forward. "Thank you?" I say, hoping like anything that I'm not next on her angry list.

In a flash, before I can even back up another step, she flies down to the ground in front of me. "Don't be afraid," she says. "Are you okay?"

She has a very serious expression. I'm not sure how to answer her question. All I can think about is how *not* okay I will be if she starts hammering my crown like she did to the stoats. "Umm . . . ," I say.

"Did they hurt you?" She takes another hop in my direction.

"No." I give my wings a flap and twist my body back and forth to make sure. "They were going to kill and eat me, but they didn't get the chance to because you . . ." I don't know what to say.

"Yes?" she says.

"Because you came along and decided they needed . . . a more open mind," I say.

The bird relaxes and looks pleased. She cocks her head to one side, and for the first time I feel like I can relax with her.

"An open mind," she says. She suddenly starts to giggle.

"I did the best I could to open their minds!" When she laughs, it sounds like "Hip, hip, hip." It is the most beautiful sound in the world. Her laughter makes me laugh too, and pretty soon we're both falling down laughing. We flap around on the ground.

After almost getting killed just a few moments before, it feels amazing to be suddenly safe with a fierce friend by my side.

"Help, Stumpy. Get this thing off me!" I say in a stoat voice.

"Whee," she says, and throws her legs up over her head with her feet pointing to the sky. "I needed a good laugh."

I look over at her from my spot in the dirt. "My name is Frank."

"I'm Mini," she says. She hops up and shakes the dust from her feathers. "Come on, let's get out of here before two stoats find their courage."

I climb to my feet, but when I look around she's gone again. She is one quick bird. Then I see her waiting for me on a rock, and I hustle after her as fast as I can. Before I can get to her, she flits ahead and waits and I follow again. We do that a few more times until she leads me to a quiet spot near a stream with moss on the ground. I settle myself onto the moss. I hadn't noticed how tired I was.

I see Mini watching me. "Did I remember to say thank you?" I say. "And by the way, why are you helping me?"

"Frank," she says, and her voice is serious. There is no more of that laughter now. "What on earth are you doing out in the forest alone?"

"Some of my duck friends told me it was a good idea," I say.

"Well, it's not." Mini hops in front of me and looks in my eyes. "You need better friends, and you need to go back home."

"I . . . I can't go home," I say. "I'm on a quest."

"What's a quest?" Mini tips her head to one side the way I've seen her do before.

"A quest is a journey to find something important," I say.

Mini stares at me for a moment. Then she says, "Tell me what's so important. Maybe I can help you and then you can go back home."

I'm not so sure I want to tell a stranger about my quest. It might seem silly . . . or weird . . . or stupid. It's starting to feel a little bit stupid even to me. But Mini did save my life. "Okay. Tell me why you saved me and I'll tell you about my quest," I say.

Mini gives me a long look, and then she scratches her foot in the dust. "I wanted to come say thank you for trying to save my family. And I wanted to apologize for attacking you. I was desperate and I wasn't thinking."

"Are your babies okay?" I say. "I mean the ones that got a chance to hatch?"

"All dead." Mini's head dips down and her feathers start to shake. Then she sways from side to side. "All dead, all dead."

"The possum?" I say.

Mini nods even while she is still swaying. "Once they find your nest, they never leave you alone. They just wait and wait for their chance."

"I'm sorry." I can't think what else to say.

After a moment, Mini shakes her head and says, "So tell me about this quest thing."

This is a bird that doesn't waste any time getting

straight to the point. Just a short bit ago I was fighting for my life, and now I'm trying to explain my quest. I take a deep breath. "My quest is to save my duck pond from a predator. A fox that is killing us."

"Duck pond?" Mini says. "Why were you in a duck pond?"

"It's my home," I say. "It's my family."

Mini looks at me for a long time without blinking. Then she says, "So you want to save a duck pond. . . ."

"My duck pond," I say.

"Okay, your duck pond. And . . . is fighting with stoats part of your quest to save your duck pond?"

"No. I'm supposed to be looking for something to protect us. Amulets." This is the part that I suddenly feel really embarrassed about now. But for some reason I want Mini to believe in my quest, so I keep going. "My friends told me about some amulets that, if I can collect them, will protect my family and all the other ducks from this fox."

Mini shakes her head slowly. I can tell it is going to be very hard to convince her. "These friends of yours, are they duck friends?" she says finally.

"Of course they are duck friends," I say.

"I thought maybe you would have some goose friends," she says.

"Goose friends?" That sounds ridiculous to me. "Why would I have goose friends?"

Mini ignores my question and just shakes her head again. "And what did your mother say when you told her about your quest . . . and your friends?"

"I want to make my mother proud," I say. "I really want to make her proud."

Mini blinks and takes a hop closer. "Your mother, she doesn't know you're out here, does she?"

I shake my head.

Thunder rolls across the sky, making me glance up. I hadn't noticed the dark clouds coming in.

When I look back, Mini is watching me. She is quiet for a moment, then she says, "Your mother is probably worried sick about you. Your feathers are starting to come in beautifully, by the way. But the forest is a dangerous place for a goose . . . or a duck. Especially if they are alone. That's why you're in trouble."

"I had to do something," I say. "It's my chance to save my pond. And maybe the other ducks will finally start being nicer to me."

"But amulets, Frank?" Mini says. "I don't think your friends—"

But I interrupt her. "Anyway," I say, "I wasn't alone. TR came with me. Have you seen her?"

Suddenly a huge crack of lightning sprays across the sky, lighting up the forest for a moment. But there is no rain following.

Mini seems nervous. She checks out the sky. Without looking at me, she says, "I might be able to help find your friend, but you have to promise me—"

Another flash of lightning, followed by a boom of thunder, covers whatever she was trying to say. Then there is another flash-boom, and this one is so close and so powerful it knocks me off my feet. I try to get up but I can't. It's as if my mind has been disconnected from my feet.

When I finally manage to get myself right side up, I'm not on the mossy patch anymore. And Mini is nowhere to be seen. Then I smell it. Smoke.

✺ Chapter 14 ✺

I don't know how I know what it is, but I know in the deepest part of me that this is smoke, and that I should be afraid. I look around and see a dead tree moving. But it's not moving. It is on fire.

Just as I know what smoke is, I know this is fire, and a surge of fear runs through me.

Suddenly, Mini flies over my head and calls to me. "There you are! Thank goodness you're okay. Frank, get out of here! It's a forest fire!"

I turn to run, but Mini yells, "No, Frank! Not that way! Follow the stream to the lake!"

I start running along the stream, and Mini flies close overhead. "Don't stop until you get to the lake! Then swim!"

"Okay!" I shout, not looking up. I didn't know there was a lake close by, but I trust Mini completely. "Try to find my turtle friend!" My webbed feet are pounding along the stream as fast as they can. I look up—Mini is gone. I don't know if she heard me or not, but I don't stop running.

Behind me I can hear the fire crackling. Another crash of thunder tries to knock me off my feet. But when the ground begins to rumble, it stops me in my tracks. A different sort of thunder coming from the ground? Then a family of deer bursts through the trees, heading straight for me.

There is nothing I can do to protect myself from their feet, but in an instant they leap past me and over the stream, and then they're gone. I can see more fire between the trees now. I start running again and I don't look back.

When I finally get to the lake, there are a few animals along the bank, nervously glancing at the fire and then at the water, waiting for their moment to swim for it. I don't wait. I just jump in.

Then I notice the dark shapes of the deer who have already decided to plunge in, and I see where they are headed. There is an island in the middle of the lake. A few animals have already made it to the island and are looking back at the fire with water dripping off their fur.

I head in that direction and then stop. Why would I swim to an island to escape the fire? I can float on top of the water all day if I need to! And it's a good thing, too. Who knows what predator on that island would love to make a snack out of me. But just as I am turning to swim in a different direction, something grabs my leg!

It tries to pull me under! I kick to get it off me, but its grip is too strong. There is no making it let go. Two ears on a furry head break the surface of the water beside me. Then I see the dark circles around the eyes. It's a raccoon!

I kick even harder to get away. The raccoon takes a breath and goes under, but it doesn't let go. I think to myself that the next time it surfaces, I'm going to use my beak to donk it right between the eyes.

But it comes up a second time making a blubbing and soft crying sound. "Please help me," it says. The raccoon goes under again, and then it pulls on my leg harder so that it can get its head out of the water for another breath. "I'm drowning. Please help me."

The last thing in the world I want to do is help a nasty old raccoon, but what choice do I have now? His grip is amazingly strong and he is not letting go.

"Okay," I say. "But you'll have to let me paddle. Grab my wing instead of my leg."

The raccoon dips his head underwater one more time and then lifts himself to grab my wing with both front paws.

"Thank you," he wheezes. "Thank you, thank you."

I start paddling for the island, which by now has even more animals standing there, staring back at the fire. Paddling with something hanging on to my wing is not easy. First of all, the weight of the raccoon tips me sideways. Second of all, it tries to make me swim in a circle. And lastly, it slows me down a lot! But if there's one thing I can do very well, it is swim.

The further I swim, the less nervous I am that this raccoon is going to try to eat me. He wheezes and burbles with every breath, like he has water in his throat. But he also pushes out a thank-you about every three breaths.

"Hey, raccoon, you don't have to keep saying thank you," I say.

"Okay," he wheezes. "My name is Flinch. And thank you."

Finally the water gets shallow near the island, and I can feel his legs drag along the ground, but still he doesn't release his grip on my wing. So I drag him completely out of the water.

"You can let go now," I say.

Flinch finally drops off and flops down on his stomach. "Thank you," he says, and closes his eyes. Then he coughs, and water comes flowing out of his mouth and nose.

The island is small and made of sand. The deer family is watching the fire from one end of the island. They are very still except when one of them stamps their feet. Along the edge there are two rabbits, a porcupine, and a family of brown furry animals, a mother and three babies. The mother is about the size of a raccoon but with no dark eye circles. I can tell from their teeth that they are not predators. In fact, there are no predators on the island . . . except for the raccoon I saved. Everyone but Flinch is watching the fire.

It grows bigger and bigger as it approaches the lake. Then it attacks the trees at the very edge. It roars and crackles. Smoke pours into the sky, and I can feel the heat all the way across the water. I wonder if more animals might join us, and I keep a lookout for a turtle. But no other animals come. I'm worried about TR.

Slowly the fire burns down and gets quieter. Then I notice the baby deer watching us. "Look, Mom," she says. "What's wrong with him?"

The mother deer glances down and takes two steps back. "Don't stare, honey. Look away, you'll have nightmares."

Nightmares? What are they talking about? But then my

eyes fall on Flinch, and I see what they mean. He is lying motionless. All the hair on one side of his body is burned off, and his skin is red and puffy. And not just on his side. All the hair on one of his back legs is burned off.

I turn away because I don't want nightmares either. I take a step back from Flinch and watch the fire on the shore like everyone else. No one is bothering anybody. We're just staring together at the fire. It's like we can't look away.

But as the sun begins to go down, so do the flames. The trees are all black at the bottom. Some are still green at the top. And on the opposite side the trees haven't been burned at all. The animals slowly start taking to the water again and swimming to the part of the forest that is still green. I didn't know rabbits could swim, but they can. So can porcupines.

Soon it is just Flinch and me and the mother deer with her child, who is trying very hard not to stare at the burned raccoon. Watching them reminds me of my own mother. Finally the mother deer turns away and her child follows. They walk with their tall legs into the water a few steps and then leap into the deep part and swim away. Now it is just me and Flinch.

I don't want to go anywhere because I want to be here when Mini comes back. I take another step away from Flinch because he looks just terrible. He still hasn't moved at all except that now he is shivering.

Then I hear him saying something. I move a little closer.

"Cold. So cold." His shivers come in waves that shake his whole body, then slow down, then violently shake him again.

Of course you're cold, I think. You don't have any fur on one side. Plus you're wet because you don't have any feathers.

"Cold," he says again. "So, so cold."

His eyes are closed, so I don't know who he thinks he is talking to. I don't even know if he knows I'm still here.

"Flinch," I say.

He doesn't move or open his eyes.

"Flinch, you're cold because your hair got burned off," I say.

"Yes," he says. "Fire. Too fast. Burning."

I can picture him running and the fire catching him. I shake my head to get the scene out of my mind. I don't want to think about this, even for an enemy . . . and—a weird thought comes to me—I'm not sure he is an enemy.

"Fire so hot," he says, and he opens his eyes for the first time since I pulled him to shore. "Night so cold."

"Well, you're all wet," I say. "Your fur is all wet."

"All wet," he says, and closes his eyes. Then a big shiver goes through his whole body from head to tail.

Before my brain even has time to think, my feet start

walking over to Flinch's side. But finally my mind catches up and makes me stop.

Sure, I can keep this raccoon warm for the night. But why? Why would I want to do anything to help a dirty, mean old raccoon? And what would Mini say if she saw me tomorrow morning, keeping an egg-eater warm . . . and alive?

"Hey," I say. "If I help you, are you going to eat me? When you get all better I mean?"

He doesn't answer. It is so dark now I can't see his face. But I can still see the terrible shivers that go down his body.

Before I can think about it anymore, I step over to his side. I'm glad it is so dark I can't see his burns. I settle down and put my body next to his, just like Mom used to do with us ducklings. He scootches closer, just like we used to do with Mother.

I warm his body. Little by little the shivers stop, and I can feel him begin to breathe regularly in his sleep. I just don't know if I'll be able to sleep myself.

❁❁ Chapter 15 ❁❁

The next morning the sun wakes me. So it turns out I did sleep. I start to stand up, but Flinch moans and moves closer, so I settle back down. I decide to wait until the sun is a little higher in the sky, a little warmer, before I get up. I just hope that Mini doesn't see the poor choice I made by saving the life of a scoundrel, an enemy of all birds.

I look down at the raccoon. His face is quiet except when his eyebrows twitch because of some dream he is having. For a moment I wonder if he is dreaming of his family. And then I wonder if maybe his mother is worried about him, which of course makes me think of my own mother. That thought makes me sad and homesick, and now I don't feel like getting up. I just sit there and think of all the families in the world.

After a while my stomach rumbles. I decide the sun is warm enough that Flinch will be fine if I get up. I stand slowly and quietly, and this time Flinch does not wake.

I swim off to look for something to eat. At the edge of the lake there are some tender water plants. I nibble the tops and find they are surprisingly tasty. But when I dig in and pull up a big clump, I see that the parts under the water are covered in snails. Yuck, I hate snails.

And that's when a thought occurs to me. I wonder if

raccoons eat snails. And if they do, then maybe this can help Flinch get better. That's when I realize I need to have a very serious talk with myself. Why do I care so much about Flinch? The only answer I can think of is that he needs help. Then one more thing occurs to me. I saved his life. It would be a shame if I saved a life only to watch him not make it.

I pull out more water plants and then swim them over to the island. Just when I get there, Flinch rolls slowly into a sitting position. I get out on the other side of the island so I can watch from a safe distance.

He tries to rise to his feet and fails twice before he finally stands up stiffly and shakes his fur. "Ouch!" he says, and sits back down.

He gingerly gets up again and limps to the water's edge and drinks deeply from the lake. Then he turns around, and that's when he sees me.

"Hello," he says. His voice is soft and rough.

"Hello," I say.

He hobbles to a spot where the sand is dry and sits down. He wavers as if he might completely fall over but steadies himself. He watches me for a moment, and I measure the space between us just in case . . . even though he doesn't seem in any shape to lunge for me.

He rubs his front feet together and smooths his whiskers. Then he stops and looks at me. "Did I remember to thank you yet?"

Last night he hardly said anything *except* thank you. But I don't mention it.

"In case I forgot, let me just say it now. Thank you, thank you, thank you so very much."

His front feet begin their rubbing again, and I can't tell if he even knows he is doing it.

"Without you, I believe I would have died," he says. "I do not know why you did this, but you have shown me such kindness—the sort I have known only from my own mother." Then he waits quietly as if he is giving me a chance to say something.

"I had no choice," I say finally. "You grabbed me."

"Ah," he says, and looks down at his front feet. "I have a very strong grip, it is true. And I was desperate." A movement in the shallow water distracts him for a moment, but he brings his eyes back to me. "I hope I did not hurt you."

I shake my head.

He looks back to the water's edge, where something is moving. I wonder if he is thinking about fishing. Not that there is any chance of him catching anything in his condition.

"Do you eat snails?" I say. "I brought you some."

"You brought me food?" He shakes his head. "Why . . . ?" He doesn't finish his question.

I wade back into the water and carefully swim the plants over to him. Judging from the stiff way he is moving,

I don't think he can rush me, but I keep a sharp eye on him just the same. "They're all over these water plants," I say.

"Thank you," he says again. He slowly takes a water plant in his front feet and pulls it toward him. "Snails are certainly good enough in a pinch."

He pops a snail into his mouth, and I hear him crunch on the shell. His teeth look sharp and dangerous. They make me think about Boss and Stumpy. He is about to toss another snail into his mouth when he stops. "I had a dream last night that my fur was wet. It was cold, and all the other animals who escaped to the island departed. Except a young goose who stayed and kept me from freezing to death in the night." He looks at me and waits for me to say something.

"I'm a duck," I say. I can't think what else to say. I still don't know for sure what made me stay . . . not only stay but keep Flinch warm in the cold night.

"A duck?" he says. "I've never seen . . . Well, no matter. Might I have the pleasure of knowing the name of the kind soul who saved my life?"

I think about this for a moment. There is no harm in telling a possibly dangerous raccoon my name, is there? "My name is Frank," I say finally.

"Well, Frank," he says, "you have shown me great kindness, and I will not rest until I can return the favor. But until then, I would like to be your friend."

✤ Chapter 16 ✤

"Do you eat birds?" I say. "Or eggs?"

Flinch looks down at his front feet, which are doing the rubbing thing again. Then he stops and turns them over as if they might answer for him. He curls and uncurls his toes. "Not anymore," he says. It's as if he's talking to his feet, but then he looks at me. "Never again from this moment forward."

I want to ask him if he used to be a bird-eater or an egg-eater. But then I decide I don't really want to know. The question now is, can I trust him? "Do you know Stumpy and Boss?" I say.

Flinch shakes his head. "Nope. Friends of yours? Any friend of yours is a friend of mine."

"Not friends," I say. "Enemies."

"Then they're my enemies too," he says.

Good answer, I think.

※

Flinch sleeps almost the whole day, and by midday his fur is completely dry. I watch for Mini, who should have come back by now, and I try not to think about all the bad things that might have happened to her . . . or TR.

Of course a part of me is dreading seeing her again because . . . what will she say when she sees me talking to Flinch?

That night I lie down on one side of the island and leave Flinch to sleep alone on his side. The stars are bright in the sky, and I watch them, waiting for sleep to come. That's when I hear it again. The moon. Memories of Mom come flooding back. I remember how it felt to share the night sounds with her. The moon song is far away, but it stirs my heart, and I feel an urge to get up to follow it. But it is gone too soon. That's when I notice that there is no moon. How strange.

In the morning Flinch struggles to his feet. He looks like he might be feeling even worse. I still can't stand seeing the parts of his body where the hair got burned off. He limps away to get a drink of water and then flops down in a sunny spot and doesn't move until the sun is at its highest place. Finally he sits up.

"Snails?" I ask.

Flinch cocks his head like he's thinking. "I don't want to sound ungrateful, because they were just what I needed, but I think I've had enough snails for a while."

"Too slimy?" I say.

"A little too slimy," he says.

"My thoughts exactly," I say.

Flinch watches me carefully for a moment. "Did you

tell me your family are ducks? I'll bet they loved snails."

"Yes, they did," I say. "I prefer grass, though." I hope he doesn't think I'm weird.

"I must say," he says, "your feathers are coming in beautifully."

It's true. Feathers cover my whole body. And when I spread my wings, I can see that my flight feathers are coming in. I suddenly feel an uncontrollable urge to flap my wings. So I do. And I feel a lightness, almost as if my body wants to rise right out of the water.

"That feels good," I say. But Flinch is looking at the water, near where he is sitting. He crouches and then leaps. Only he barely gets off the ground. In fact, he doesn't even make it to the water. And when he turns away, he is limping even worse. "Ouch," he says. "That hurt." He flops down in the soft sand. "Ooh, my goodness that hurt." He puts his front paws over his eyes.

I swim over to look at what he was trying to catch. There is something on the lake floor, not far under the water. It looks like some sort of water beetle with pincers and a flat tail. "What is it?" I ask.

He uncovers his eyes to see what I'm looking at. "It's a crawdad," he says, "and they're delicious."

"I doubt it," I say. But I dive my head under, grab the crawdad in my beak, and then fling it onto the sand. Flinch stumbles over to it and bites it before dropping it.

He looks at me with his eyes wide. "I can't believe you did that!" he shouts. "That was amazing! Can you get another one?"

I paddle around the shore of the island, looking. Flinch limps, right along with me, and as soon as I see a second one, I flip it up onto the sand. Only the crawdad never lands. Flinch catches it in the air, bites it, and puts it next to the first one. After two more, no other crawdads are careless enough to be in sight.

"Four nice fat crawdads!" says Flinch. "This is the best breakfast ever."

"Enjoy," I say.

"Are you sure you don't want to join me?" he asks. "They're delicious."

"No they're not," I say, and go to find my own meal. But as I'm swimming off, I realize that no matter how much I might promise myself to keep my distance from Flinch, I can't seem to remember to do it for very long.

❁

Flinch wakes up the next morning before I've even had breakfast. He stretches and stretches and then shakes the sand out of his fur. It is clear to me he is feeling better. But when he tries to walk, he still looks stiff.

He sees me watching and sits down and rubs his front

paws. He looks around like there might be something he wants to say.

I wait. I think he might want to talk to me about food. I've been on the lookout for crawdads, but the ones near the island seem to have gotten the message and disappeared.

"I woke up with a question," he says finally.

I don't say anything.

"I realize I've been selfish and have not asked you where you were going when you so kindly saved my life in the lake." He isn't rubbing his front paws anymore. "You seem a little young to be on your own," he says. He waits quietly.

I give a big sigh because the story of my quest hasn't gone over very well with anyone I've met. But I decide to try one more time, and I tell him the whole thing—about my family, the Fab Four, TR and Mini, the killer fox, and Stumpy and Boss.

"Stoats, yikes," says Flinch. When I'm finished, he doesn't tell me my quest is dumb.

"Amulets," he says, nodding. "That's not really a raccoon thing, but I wonder if I can help you with your quest. Are you allowed to have help?"

I think about this for a moment. I never thought about it before, but I've already had help from TR and Mini.

"Nobody said anything about doing it alone without help," I say. "What do you have in mind?"

Flinch starts rubbing his front paws again, and he cocks his head to one side like he's thinking . . . or trying to remember. "I don't usually pay much attention to these things, but I may have passed by some bones and teeth in my travels."

I feel so appreciative I hardly know what to say. "Thank you," I say, but it just doesn't seem like enough. A feeling of hope that I haven't felt since the start of my quest floats like a bubble from my leg bones all the way to the top of my head. "Thank you, thank you, thank you."

Flinch smiles. "You are sounding like me the first time we met."

❈

That night, Flinch and I look up at the stars side by side. Neither of us says anything, and listening to the frogs croak out their songs and watching the reflection of tiny points of light on the surface of the lake and feeling hope in my heart makes it seem like there is something magical in this place.

Then Flinch clears his throat like maybe he's nervous, and instantly everything feels less magical. "I wanted to talk to you about something," he says. "A little something."

I keep looking up at the stars in hopes that the magic feeling can come back. "How little?" I say softly.

"Well . . . ," he says, "maybe not so little."

I turn away from the stars because there is no magic left, and I look at Flinch. In the darkness I can only see his outline. I'm pretty sure he's going to tell me my quest is dumb.

He clears his throat again.

"Just say whatever you're going to say," I tell him.

"I'm speaking as a friend," he says. "I would never mention this except that you're the best friend I've ever had."

He stops talking, and I try to let in what he is telling me. A raccoon and a duck, best friends? Does that even make sense?

"But I need to speak up," he says. "Have you seen your reflection in the water? Your color? Your size? Your shape?"

I look away. The truth is I have seen my reflection, and it confuses me.

"Frank," he says, "you are not a duck."

I don't answer him. At first the words don't sink in. Then I feel a cold current coming up from my legs that wants to take over my whole body. Somehow this feels like a conversation I've been having my whole life, only I can't remember exactly when. I'm angry . . . and that is a very familiar feeling too. A coldness rises up, into my bones, heavy as a stone.

I take a deep breath. "Why would you say that?" In the next instant I know I don't want to hear another word from

Flinch. "Don't answer!" I say.

There is another feeling now. A feeling like . . . like I've known that what Flinch is saying is true even though I didn't ever want to believe it. I look down at my wing. I can't see much in the light from the stars. But my duck family is . . . all white. Everyone was white from top to bottom . . . except for feet and beak. My wing feathers are gray . . . not white.

The thoughts in my head are buzzing so loudly now I can hardly hear the frogs. "So . . . what am I?"

"A goose." Flinch clears his throat again. "Frank, I didn't mean to . . ."

"Please . . . just be quiet," I say. "Don't say anything right now. I . . . I just need some time. . . ." I can't think what to say. I've never felt so alone and so glad to have a

friend at my side at the same time.

Thankfully, Flinch doesn't say anything else all night. And how do I know that? Because I don't get a wink of sleep. The word "goose" just keeps bumping around in my head. What does a goose look like? Have I ever seen a goose? I mean up close? No. That means I don't even know what I will look like when I'm full grown.

And what do geese do? How do they make their lives? I'm pretty sure they don't eat snails. But how do they act? And how am I going to learn how I'm supposed to act? Are geese kind? Do they hate intruders? Will other geese like me, even though I wasn't hatched in their clans?

These are the questions that do not let me sleep.

✣ Chapter 17 ✣

"I just have to mention it again," Flinch says the next morning as I float by. "Your feathers seem thicker and more developed every day. Are your flight feathers longer today than yesterday, or is that my imagination?"

I figure that Flinch is just trying to say something nice to make up for the things he said last night. But I stretch out a wing and look anyway. And it's true! The joy I feel just can't be kept inside. I lift my wings and flap. In fact, I pound the air. To my surprise my body comes completely clear of the water. I'm so shocked when I look down that I stop flapping and sink back to the lake like a stone. "Did you see that?" I say.

"You're almost a flier!" says Flinch. "Soon you'll be flying all around this lake!"

I fold my wings and float for a moment because a thought has come to me. Flinch gets quiet too and seems to know that he should just let me think for a bit. All my life I imagined being able to fly. But I always saw myself flying as a duck. Who's going to teach me to fly like a goose?

"Frank?" says Flinch finally. "Ready to try again?"

"Sure," I say. And I think to myself that whether I fly like a goose or a duck . . . or something in between, it's going to feel great to be a flier.

I flap again and notice my feet aren't quite coming free of the water. I decide to try harder. I flap away from the island. My feet are still dragging. After a short rest I flap back. Then I flap my way around the island, and after that I turn around and go the other direction.

Flinch is jumping up and down on all four feet. By this time I'm exhausted but filled with excitement. I need to eat and get some energy so I can try again, but first I swim close to the island because I have to tell Flinch what is on my mind.

He lifts one paw over and over in the air, and he's making noises that aren't even words and sound like "Eeeeyow!" and "Zowee!" I stand in front of him and wait. I appreciate the support, but I have something important to say. Finally he seems to get the point and stops making those noises.

"I want to tell you that I get it now that I'm not a duck," I say. "I get it that I'm a goose." I wait for him to say something, but he just watches me. "You probably think I'm stupid. You probably knew that you were a raccoon from the day you were born, and you probably think that it's dumb that I . . ."

"I don't think you're stupid," he says.

"Anyway," I say. I act calm even though his words mean the world to me. "It's complicated for me because my family are ducks. But I don't want to talk about it anymore—I just wanted to let you know." I start to swim away, but then I think of one more thing I want to say. I look back at Flinch. "And thank you."

I swim off to get some breakfast, but Flinch calls out to me. "Maybe I'll meet your family someday," he says.

I turn around. "That's a terrible idea," I call back. "They would hate you."

"Oh," he says. "Okay."

After breakfast I practice and then rest, practice and then rest. While I'm resting I say to myself, "Goose, not duck." Sometimes the words feel sad. Other times they feel exciting but a little lonely. Flinch does a happy dance every time I come close to the island, and then I don't feel so alone.

By the next day I find I can run on top of the water while flapping and then glide a short ways. But because I don't know how to turn yet, I have to make a crash landing. Sometimes water goes up my nose, and I hope Flinch isn't watching. He spends part of the day prowling the edge of the island for crawdads.

When I'm ready, I point myself toward the island and flap my wings to take off again. I make another crash landing in front of the island, but this time I avoid getting water up my nose.

Flinch hops up and down on his hind feet. "That was

fantastic!" he shouts, even though I'm practically close enough to touch him. "You were flying!"

"I was gliding," I correct him. This doesn't stop him from dancing. I climb out of the water and onto the island and settle down. Flinch's dancing takes him in a circle all around me.

I must admit, it feels extremely good to be celebrated like this.

Then suddenly there is a screaming sound, and something is zooming around Flinch's head.

"Ow, ow, OUCH!" he screams. "Please stop!"

This time I know exactly what it is. "Mini, no!" I shout. "This is Flinch. He's my friend!"

Mini does stop for a moment. But she is not one to take someone else's words to heart very quickly, so she gives Flinch two or three more raps on the top of his head.

"Ouch!" yells Flinch. "Get off!"

But Mini has already stopped and flits down to the ground. "You know this raccoon?" she says. "And you trust him?" She tilts her head to one side and looks at Flinch.

I can tell she isn't going to be easily convinced. Flinch is rubbing his crown.

"Yes," I say, and I move over next to Flinch to prove it. "This raccoon is my friend. We've been staying here together on this island while I was waiting for you. He's going to help me find some bones."

"I think she already found a bone," says Flinch. "Right on the top of my head. Wow, that hurts."

"You're friends?" Mini looks back and forth from me to Flinch. "Frank, I don't like this one bit. It isn't making any sense."

"I know," I say. "But I saved his life. He was burned in the fire, and then he was drowning in the lake, but I swam him over to this island."

I can tell from the way Mini is looking at me that she still doesn't understand.

"Actually he grabbed me to keep from drowning," I say. "So I didn't really have a choice. But I really did save his life."

"Let me see if I understand," says Mini. "This creature gets himself burned, grabs you, and forces you to swim him to safety. And you reward him with your friendship?" She squints and hops toward Flinch. He takes a step back and covers his head with his front paws.

"Mini," I say, "stop that. Look, I'm not asking you to like him, or even trust him. Just please don't attack him."

Flinch takes a very small step forward. "If you give me a chance," he says, "I will prove myself to you."

"That will never happen," says Mini. "If Frank says not to attack you, then I won't. But I will not let down my guard around you." Then she turns to me. "I'm sorry I took so long. It was not easy tracking down your turtle friend. . . ."

"You found TR!" I shout.

"Yes, I finally found TR," says Mini. "And now that I've found you, I can bring her to you."

"Oh, thank you, thank you, thank you!" I say. "Yes please!"

"In that case, I should fly off and get her." Mini glares at Flinch, who is rubbing his front paws again. "But that means leaving you alone with him," she says.

I stamp my foot. "Mini, I've been alone with Flinch for days and days. Stop worrying about me and go get TR."

Mini nods. "Okay," she says.

"Oh, but before you go, Mini," I say, and I open up my wings to their full glory. "What do you think of these?"

Mini relaxes for the first time, and then she breaks out in that high-pitched laugh I love so much. "Hip, hip, hip," she laughs. "I bet you thought those feathers would never grow in!"

"Yup, you're right!" I say. "But they did and I'm a flier now!"

"Wow," says Mini. "That's fantastic! And by the way, you're huge!"

"I know," I say. "And I also figured out that I'm a goose, not a duck. Flinch helped me."

Mini nods and looks at Flinch as if in a new way. I hope she is starting to soften her feelings toward him. "That's no small thing," she says finally. "And congratulations."

I lower my wings, and Mini gives her tail a twitch, which probably means she is ready to fly off.

"It will take TR a while to get here," she says, "so I'd better go and get her started."

"Wait, I just had an idea," I say. "Tell TR to meet me back at the duck pond. I'm going to be headed that way soon anyhow."

"Are you sure?" says Mini.

"Flinch knows where I can find the amulets I'm looking for," I say. "And then I'll be headed back. Will you wait for me at the duck pond too? I might need help."

"Done," says Mini. "See you at the duck pond."

And before I can even see which way she goes, she's gone.

Chapter 18

The next morning, before Flinch is awake, I swim out on a very calm, clear lake and look at myself in the water. There is no wind and no sound. I take a deep breath, flap my wings, and fly. I really fly. Low at first, but then gradually higher. I'm not sure why I can do today what I couldn't do yesterday, but today I'm a real flier.

When I'm at the tops of the small trees, I level out and just work on smoothing out my turns. I also practice gliding for a little while and then flapping again. I'm not even very tired when I decide to come in for a water landing. And it is perfect. When I touch down, I push forward a small wave, and then everything is quiet again. My wave gently tips up on the island, and I see that Flinch is awake.

I know he has been watching me, but he isn't jumping around or cheering this time. Instead he punches the air with his little paw and then sits down to watch me again.

Suddenly, out of the pure silence, I hear the moon. Only now I know deep down it was never the moon at all.

The sound that thrilled me when I was a duckling— or . . . a gosling—was voices on the wind. Voices on the wing. Voices that were calling me into myself before I even knew what they were.

In another moment a band of geese glides in over the trees and down to the lake, calling to each other. I can't take my eyes off them. They are beautiful, and graceful. And noisy. They splash down, and their calls get softer until they are just floating quietly together at the far end of the lake.

I paddle around to the other side of the island. Flinch looks at the geese and back at me. "Go say hi," he says.

"I can't," I whisper. "I don't know what to say."

"Just go introduce yourself," says Flinch. "Tell them your name and just be friendly."

"I'm embarrassed. And I want them to like me, but what if they think I'm weird?" I glare at Flinch. "I don't think I could handle it if they think I'm weird."

"You're not weird," Flinch says.

A goose is swimming our way. Flinch hunches away from me, and I look down like I'm searching for something in the water.

"Hello," says the goose as she swims up. She glances curiously at Flinch, but it's clear she doesn't fear him. She is so elegant and strong-looking I can hardly breathe at first. I've never seen anything so beautiful before.

"Hello," I say. I'm so shy all of a sudden. I desperately want this goose to like me and to not go away. I just don't have any idea what to say.

"Would you like to come meet my family?" she says.

And my heart almost melts. I nod because I'm not sure
I can control my voice. As soon as she turns around to lead
the way, I look back at Flinch with my eyes wide. He waves
me forward with his front paws.

I swim after her, and soon I'm among her group. My
mind is filled with questions, and I don't feel like I can ask
any of them. Will these geese test me? Are they staying for
a while? Where did they come from? And . . . do they think
I'm weird?

The goose who invited me over turns and says, "My
name is Camilia. This is my mom, Tendriya, my brother
Cassian, and my sister Eliana."

Each of them nods gracefully as they are introduced.

I try to nod back just as gracefully, but I'm pretty sure I'm making a mess of it. It's my turn to introduce myself, and a bad feeling sits in the pit of my stomach. First of all, my name isn't half as nice as their names. For sure they're going to think I'm a weirdo.

"My name is Frank," I say. "And it is very nice to meet you."

They look at me, and there is an awkward silence. Did I say something stupid already?

"Um . . ." The brother, Cassian, swims a little closer. "Why do you talk like that? You sound like—"

"Cassian!" The mother, Tendriya, swims in front of Cassian, making him back up. "Don't be rude! Do you think every goose came from the same cornfield where you grew up?"

I'm wishing I knew what a cornfield was and if that is where all geese live.

Cassian looks down and then up at his mother. After another awkward silence, he looks at me. "I would like to apologize," he says. "I keep forgetting that we geese live and fly from all parts of the globe. Frank, I hope you will forgive me."

"That's better," says Tendriya.

Camilia giggles but turns away before her mother can say anything.

"That's okay," I say. I really want to ask what a globe is, but I don't.

Eliana swims up to me. She is smaller than her brother and sister, and she has an open, friendly way about her. "We're on our migration," she says.

Another word I've never heard before. I struggle to keep the feeling that I'm stupid down in my chest.

Eliana continues. "We started early this year because it's my first migration and I fly a little slower than the others. But I'm learning, and I'm getting stronger!"

She looks at her mother like she has a question, and her mother nods.

Eliana bends her neck low and looks up into my eyes. "We couldn't help noticing that you're alone, and we want to know if you'd like to join us."

My heart leaps. An invitation to fly with geese! To go where they go, know what they know, learn to talk like them and feel like I belong! And then I remember my quest. "I can't!" I blurt out.

"You would be more than welcome," says Cassian. "We are happy to fly at whatever pace is best for everyone."

"That means they don't mind flying slow for me, because I'm the slowest," says Eliana.

"Come with us," says Camilia. "We don't like to think of you all alone."

I gulp and try to find my words. "I'm very grateful for your concern, but I can't, because I'm on a . . ." I almost say I'm on a quest, and I can just imagine the questions then. What's a quest? Why are you trying to save a bunch of ducks? What do you mean that's your family?

I think fast. "I'm on a scouting mission for my family. They want me to find the best way for . . ." What was that word?

"The migration?" says Camilia.

"Yes! The migration!" I say.

"Well, that is very brave of you," says Tendriya. "We wish you the best of luck, don't we, kids?"

All the younger geese nod.

"It was nice to meet you," says Cassian. "Maybe we'll meet again at the gathering place."

"Yes, I hope so," I say. "I very much hope so." I have a terribly sad feeling in my chest now that probably the nicest family of geese in the whole world will fly out of my life forever.

"We'll be leaving at the first light of dawn," says Tendriya. "Let us know if you change your mind. You're always welcome."

✤

"So how did it go?" asks Flinch when I get back to the island.

"They were really nice," I say.

"Oh yeah?" he says. "Well, that's because you're a great guy. What did I tell you?"

"Thanks, Flinch," I say.

⚛ Chapter 19 ⚛

I don't want to wake up early the next morning. I don't want to hear them taking off and calling encouragement to each other. I don't want to see them disappearing over the tops of the trees. But I do. Then I tuck my head under my wing so I don't have to face the day. I can't express how sad I am in the morning silence. I don't even feel like going off to look for breakfast.

Flinch starts humming from the time he wakes up. I finally lift my head to see him searching for crawdads in the shallows near the little island. Every once in a while he stops and sniffs the air. Finally he makes his way over to where I'm still moping.

"Well," he says, "that quest is waiting. And those bones aren't going to find themselves, so we'd better get moving."

"We," I say. I roll that small word around in my mouth. I'm not alone. I might not have a goose clan to belong to, but I have something else. A friend.

"Unless we're not doing the quest anymore." He scratches behind one of his ears. "Did you change your mind?"

"No," I say. "I didn't change my mind. I'm still . . . I mean, we're still doing the quest."

"All right then." Flinch rubs his front feet together. "Let's get a move on. There's no more crawdads left around here anyway."

"But how are you going to get off the island?" I ask.

"Swim, of course. Not everyone can fly, you know."

"You can swim?"

"Of course I can swim!" He stops rubbing his feet. "All raccoons can . . . Oh, I get it. The last time you saw me swimming . . ."

"You mean drowning?" I say.

"Yeah, drowning," he says. "But that raccoon was burned and almost dead. Look at this one!"

He stands up and turns around. The places where his fur was burned off have fuzz on them now.

"All better," he says.

It's not all better, but it's a big improvement. I notice that there is a spot on his leg that is still just bare skin. I wonder if the fur will ever grow back like normal. But the skin looks healthy.

"See you on the other side." Flinch plunges into the water and paddles so strongly that I can hardly believe this is the same creature I saved from the lake. I swim after him and soon cruise past him.

"Show-off!" he says.

When he reaches the shore, he shakes himself and then hunch-runs in a way that only raccoons can, straight into the burned-out forest. Some grass and a few flowers are already coming up from the ashes. "Come on!" he shouts over his shoulder. "I'm pretty sure I remember where I saw some bones."

I decide to half walk, half fly. Flinch is not graceful, but he can still run a lot faster than a goose.

After a while he stops beside a stream. The trees around us here weren't touched by the fire. He sniffs this way and that. I glide up and land beside him.

"What are you doing?" I ask. I'm pretty sure that not even a raccoon can smell old bones.

Flinch looks at me. "What do you think I'm doing?" he says.

"Surely you can't smell bones," I say.

"Everything has a smell if you're a raccoon. Even sunshine has a smell. But bones? Definitely."

Flinch is practically out of sight before I can think of anything else to say.

I catch up as he is picking at something on the ground.

"What is it?" I say. "I mean, what was it?"

"Hmm . . . not sure." Flinch stops picking and circles around it.

I can definitely see bones—most of them yellow and not very big, and some old dry skin with little patches of hair sticking to it.

"I got it!" Flinch puts one paw up in the air. "I know what this is. It's a mole. Um, I mean it *was* a mole."

"A mole?" I say. "What's a mole?"

"An underground hole digger," says Flinch. "A tunnel digger. But just to be nice, he came up above the ground to die."

I walk around the thing that used to be a mole. It is very hard to tell what it might have looked like when it was alive. There is a part that used to be the head, but the eyes are gone. There are two large, flat, yellow teeth sticking out of its face.

"Is this a predator?" I say. "Because I need to get a bone, tooth, and claw from a predator."

Flinch puts a front paw to his chin and looks thoughtful for a moment. Then he lifts up his paw. "Definitely a predator!" he says.

I stare at Flinch. "I never heard of a predator that lives underground. And look at those teeth. They're not even sharp."

"Oh, they're sharp, all right!" Flinch reaches down and touches a tooth and then jerks his paw away as if it cut him. "Ouch!" he says.

"Flinch, stop messing around," I say, and I watch him put his pretend-cut paw up to his mouth.

"Ta-da!" Flinch shows me his paw. "I'm a fast healer."

"Very tricky," I say. "Seriously, though, that's not a predator. I need a bone, a tooth, and a claw from a predator."

Flinch picks up a long black claw. "Just look at these claws."

"They're for digging!" I'm practically yelling now because Flinch doesn't seem to get the point. "Those aren't for killing! Moles probably eat roots. They don't hunt."

"You wouldn't say that if you were a worm," says Flinch.

"Moles eat worms?" I say.

"Yes, they do." Flinch sits up and rubs his front paws together.

I narrow my eyes at him, daring him to lie to me. "How do you know that?"

"I don't know." He shrugs. "Raccoons just know things."

"Now you're just making stuff up."

"Nope," says Flinch. "They track those worms down." He crouches like he is on the hunt and then crawls slowly forward and acts like he's digging. "And they wait for just the right moment . . . and then they attack!" He pounces and makes a slashing motion with one of his front paws. "And then they eat those worms from head to tail." He makes it look like he's shoving a really long worm into his mouth. "Deadly, deadly predators," he says, and licks his lips.

I make another circle around the dead mole, nudging

Flinch aside when he won't move out of the way. I notice how much bigger than him I am.

"Okay," I say. "How are we going to remove a bone, a tooth, and a claw?"

"Watch me," he says. He wiggles and twists the long dark claws one by one, and I think about how there is no way I could do what he is doing for me. Finally he finds a loose claw and pulls it right off. It is small but sharp. Then he reaches into the mouth, and I can guess he is doing the same thing with the teeth.

I turn away because I'm starting to feel sick. When I turn back, he has all three things in a line—a claw, a bone, and a long yellow tooth. And for a moment I just stand there and look at them.

"That's fantastic," I say in a soft voice. But actually they don't look like anything special. I guess I expected to feel something big, something important. I wait to see if my instincts might start speaking inside my head. Nothing happens. But maybe if I take them back to the pond with me, someone can help figure out how they work.

"I don't know what I would have done if I didn't find you, Flinch."

"And I don't know what I would have done if you didn't find me," he says. Then he looks up at the sky for a quick moment. "Actually I do know." He looks back at me. "I'd be dead, come to think of it."

"Can you . . . ?" A thought comes to me. "Will you come back to my home pond with me . . . and can you carry those things?"

"Yup." He picks them up in his front paws and lifts them up to show me.

I shake my head. "All this time, I never thought about getting them back to the pond. I don't have any way to carry things. What was I thinking? And what was Derrick thinking when he sent me on this quest?"

I look at Flinch. "Can you carry them and still walk?"

"I think so," he says. He carefully works the amulets into one front paw and then starts walking on three legs. If he walked a little funny before, he really walks funny now. But I don't laugh. I just feel grateful.

"Okay," I say. "Let's go. Do you know where we're going?"

"The duck pond?" Flinch switches the amulets into his other front paw. He drops the bone and has to pick it back up. "I sure do."

"How do you know that?"

"Like I said before, raccoons just know things. We slip around, we listen, we talk, we figure stuff out."

We walk for a while. On three legs, Flinch can still climb over fallen trees and scamper along forest trails faster than I can on two. The forest is thick here, too thick for me to fly through, so Flinch has to pause and wait for me sometimes just like I used to wait for TR.

We stop beside another stream to rest. I nibble at the grasses on the bank, and Flinch lays the amulets carefully on the ground and splashes around in the water until he comes up with a fish.

"Ha!" he shouts. "I got one!"

"How did you do that?" I say.

"Strong grip," says Flinch. "Very grabby paws. Nothing gets away from these paws."

He sits beside the stream, picks the fish into pieces, and washes each bite before he eats it. Finally there's nothing left but fish bones, the tail, and the head.

"Ready to go?" I say.

He rubs his paws together like he's still washing his food even though there is no more to wash. "I have an idea," he says. "I think you should fly, and we can meet up at the pond. I can go faster than you on land, and there's no reason why you shouldn't just make it easier on yourself."

He waits for me to reply, but I can't think what to say. I just feel so grateful that Flinch is doing all the things I can't do.

"Take to the wing?" he says. "Just tell me where you want to meet up."

"There's a stream that feeds the pond," I say. "It comes out of the forest. Let's meet by the stream just inside the tree line. Don't lose the amulets, okay?"

"Not a chance," he says. "See you soon."

✤ Chapter 20 ✤

When the pond comes into view over the trees, I fly higher. I can't keep my heart from doing flip-flops in my chest. I've worked so hard to be back . . . home? It feels funny to think that word now. I don't know where home is anymore. I wanted so much to be a duck, to be accepted, to belong.

The ducks in the pond below me are not my family, I tell myself. Not even my species. And yet they are the only family I have. Except for my friends. And they aren't really family. Actually they aren't my species either. What a mess.

Then I remember the fox. This is not about me and my feelings. I make a turn and fly just a little bit lower, hoping that no one looks up. I don't want to be noticed until I have the amulets. I don't know what I'll say to my friends . . . or the ducks I thought were my friends. Hi, I'm the one you used to call ugly and beat up on? But here are those amulets you wanted? Oh, and by the way, just try to donk my head now . . . if you can even reach it.

I look down and don't see any sign of the fox.

An updraft presses on the underside of my wings, and I let the warm breeze push me higher and away. I float over the forest and out of sight of the pond. What pulls me back here so strongly? I ask myself. Family. That word just rings and rings in my brain. The breeze pushes me once again over the pond.

I don't know if they will even recognize me. . . . How could they? And speaking of recognizing things, from this new point of view, nothing at my old pond looks the same . . . and everything looks the same. I've never seen the nesting sites from above, but somehow I know exactly what I'm looking at. After circling twice, I find the stream that feeds the pond and land just inside the trees.

I miss my friends, my real friends, TR, Mini, and Flinch. Not Derrick and Donna and the others. If they were never my real friends, are the amulets real? Did they send me on a fake quest just to get rid of me? No one could be that mean, could they?

I consider what to do with the amulets. Who should I give them to? The more I think about it, the more I'm convinced they're probably fake. But what if they're not? I worked so hard finding them. Was it all just a waste of time?

I look down, and I feel sure there used to be more ducks. Then I see movement on the bank. I fly closer. There's something else—leaves scattered on the ground, as if a storm has just blown through. Oh no! I bank away when I realize what I have just seen. Death. Those aren't leaves—those are feathers. The bodies of not one but two ducks are lying in ruin on the ground. And the movement? That is a fox feeding on the last remains of one of my friends or family members.

I can hardly stay airborne. I have to concentrate to keep my wings out because I just want to fold up in a ball and mourn.

I guide myself to where the trees once again look familiar, and I float under the branches near the big log. My friends are all there, chatting away with each other. They turn to greet me.

"Hi, Frank, we were worried . . . ," starts Mini, but she stops when she sees my face. I can't pretend that nothing is wrong.

I choke out the words about what I've seen. "The fox . . . he's still here and still killing. This is my family, and . . . I've got to do something."

"I brought the amulets," says Flinch. The bone, tooth, and claw are in front of him on the ground. "What should we . . . ?"

"I don't know what to do with the amulets," I say. "I don't even know how they're supposed to work."

"Amulets and bones and—" says TR.

I put a big flight feather over TR's mouth and she stops talking. Then I lean my neck all the way down and put my cheek on the top of her scaly head. It's not easy to hug a turtle, so this is the best I can do. "TR," I say, "I've missed you so much and I was worried about you every day we were apart. It's so good to see you again, but if you say 'Blah, blah, blah,' I'm going to freak out."

"Okay," she says. "Sorry. And I missed you too."

"I'll just take these and see if someone knows how they work," I say. "But I think I need to do this myself. I can't ask you guys to face down a fox that isn't even your enemy."

I begin picking up the amulets in my beak. It isn't easy, holding more than one thing. I can grab two, but when I try to pick up the third, one always falls out.

Finally I get all three to stay, but before I can spread my wings again, Mini flies in front of me. "Frank, you can't go down there and face a fox with just yourself and your amulets."

The bone falls out of my mouth, and I drop the tooth and claw. They taste terrible.

"She's right," says Flinch. "You have the amulets, but you need a plan, and you need us. And . . . I hate to say this, but . . . we might need to fight. You're the biggest one. But you don't have grabby paws. Let me help you."

"And I have a beak that can be a weapon when I can surprise my enemy. Right, Flinch?" says Mini.

Flinch groans and rubs the top of his head.

"And I have a turtle mouth," says TR. "When I get ahold of something, like, let's say a tail, no one can make me let go until I feel like it."

I fold my wings and look at Flinch, who is rubbing his front feet again. "Grabby paws?" I say.

He stops his washing motion and makes a show of swiping at the air with both front paws, as if he is chasing a mosquito . . . or getting a spiderweb out of his face. He suddenly grabs an unfortunate imaginary enemy and wrings its neck. Then he stops and flashes his front paws at me with his toes splayed apart. "Super grabby," he says.

"And I have a hard shell," says TR. "No fox is ever going to bite through this shell."

"We're going to beat this fox with grabby paws? And a hard shell?" I shift from one foot to the other. "And a sharp little beak? This fox is a cold-blooded killer!"

"Exactly," says Mini. "And he is killing your family. Oh, and he'll kill you too if he gets the chance."

"Maybe we can outsmart him." I look into the forest. "So . . . what's his weakness?" No one says anything, so I keep talking. "He's stronger than us, has bigger teeth than us, and might be smarter than any of us . . . but . . ." I look around at my little team. "Is he smarter than all of us put together?"

"And does he think he's smarter than he really is?" Mini bobs her head up and down and side to side excitedly.

"And don't forget," I say, "my brother and sister said they would always be there for me whenever I need them . . . if . . . if they're still alive." Saying this out loud makes my heart sink right down into my webbed feet, and I realize that I'm a lot more worried than I let myself feel. If something happened to Darryl or Darlene . . . or Mom, I don't think I could go on.

"We need everyone," says Mini. "But you can talk to them later. Right now we need to come up with a plan."

We spend the rest of the day huddled in a group—heads to the center, tails to the outside. I only bring up the amulets one more time, and I glare at TR so she doesn't forget about not saying Blah, blah, blah. But actually I am starting to think about them less and less.

We don't completely agree about our plan at first, and Flinch keeps asking when he should put his grabby paws around the neck of the fox.

"Raccoons don't back down to anyone," he says.

"We are not going to defeat him by strangulation," I say for the third time. "For one thing, that is not our strength. . . ."

"Maybe it's not *your* strength," says Flinch, "since you don't even have paws with strong toes. You have no idea how strong these toes are."

"And second of all . . ." I do my best to avoid Mini's eyes since I'm afraid she might break out laughing in spite of the grave danger we are facing down. "We need to figure out how to put the fox in a place where he is at a disadvantage . . . someplace where he is uncomfortable." I look around at my friends. "Ideas, anyone?"

"Easy," says TR.

This is a really annoying thing to hear because, first of all, it isn't easy. And second of all, if it was easy, TR should have spoken up a while ago. But TR has been rather silent ever since I asked her not to make fun of the amulets. So when she says this, we all get quiet and look at her. TR reaches her surprisingly long and wrinkled neck out, opens her mouth, and clamps onto a clump of grass. Twisting her head this way and that way, she finally yanks the grass out and starts chewing it. Very slowly.

I watch for two more chews. "You can't just say 'easy' and then take a mouthful of food. What's easy? Tell us your idea."

"Mff, grrrg, larrp . . . ," says TR.

"Actually," I say, "finish swallowing first. That's just gross." I turn my head so I don't have to watch the green goop in TR's mouth.

After the last gulp goes down, TR slowly pushes in

between me and Flinch on her way to the stream and puts her head in to drink. All eyes follow. Finally she raises her head and splashes one of her front feet in the water. "Not everyone is comfortable in this," she says.

✦✦✦ Chapter 21 ✦✦✦

We have our plan, and somehow it doesn't include amulets at all in the end. I feel so strange about that. I spent so much time searching for them . . . but maybe ducks need amulets. And a goose needs friends. What are we going to do, knock the fox on the head with the bone? Scratch him with the claw? I can see now it is going to take more than good luck to defeat this enemy.

"Okay, does everyone understand what they're supposed to do?" says Mini.

When there aren't any questions, Mini nods to me and I take to the air. I'm nervous. No—I'm downright scared. But I tell myself that it's time for action.

I land softly at one end of the pond. All the ducks are clustered on the other side, so I don't have to talk to anyone for now. But I can feel the eyes of a whole duck clan on me. I remember how much they hate strangers on their pond.

I look over at them, trying not to stare. Is Mom there somewhere? Is she . . . still alive? My heart sinks again. I paddle a little closer and sure enough three of them break from the pack and swim over to me. I know them instantly. It's Derrick, Dexter, and Dennis from the gang of teenagers who sent me on that crazy quest. I wonder where Donna is.

"Hey, just wanted to let you know this is a duck pond," says Derrick.

"Yeah, it's a duck pond, not a goose pond," says Dennis.

"So?" I look down on the three of them. I can't believe how much bigger than them I am. They seem nervous and paddle backward a bit. I paddle ever so slightly forward.

"So," says Dexter, "you can stay and rest here a while, but . . ."

"Yeah, you can rest here a *short* while," says Derrick. He backs up a little further. "But then you should be moving along."

I let the pond waves bob me up and down, and I think about how things have changed. I used to be the little guy. Now I'm wondering what these three could possibly do to me if I decided I wanted to stay. "I might want to make friends with the ducks on this pond," I say.

"We don't need any friends," says Dexter. He says this really fast and really strongly.

"Yeah, we have all we need right here," says Dennis.

And suddenly I know for certain that everything the duck gang ever told me was a lie. It was a lie that they were my friends when I was young. But even more important, the whole quest was a lie too. The story about bones and teeth being amulets was nothing but a lie.

More than anything in the world, what I really want to do right now is donk all three of these bullies on the head ten times each. But I don't. I have a fox to defeat.

"There is one thing that could make me move along sooner rather than later," I say.

The three ducks look at each other.

"I have a message for a couple of ducks who used to live here," I say. "Maybe they still live here." If they're still alive, I think.

They stare at me, and I wonder how strange this must sound to them. But I don't have a better idea. "Are Darryl and Darlene . . . are they still around?" I say.

The three birds look at each other again. If they can't

figure out who I am by now, they are dumber than I thought.

"We might know a couple of ducks with those names," says Derrick.

It doesn't seem like they know who I am, and I don't want to tell them . . . yet. That would create a distraction that I don't need right now. But someday I'll tell them that I'm onto them with their meanness and their lies. Their stupid amulets and quest could have gotten me killed.

But for now I need them to deliver my message. "Go tell them I need to talk to them."

They look at each other and act super confused for a little longer but finally swim back toward the clan. I swim in the other direction so that if Darryl and Darlene actually show up, we can have some privacy.

And sure enough, Darryl and Darlene come skimming over the water in no time and splash down near me. I'm not sure I would have recognized them if I wasn't expecting them. I can only imagine how different I must look.

"Are you . . . are you Frank?" says Darlene before I can put them at ease.

"Frank, is it really you?" says Darryl.

"Yup!" I tell them. "How did you know it was me?"

"We've been waiting so long for you to come back!" They both start swimming around me, quacking like crazy.

"Stop," I say. "You're making me dizzy!"

They stop, but Darlene swims up so close she's

practically climbing on top of me. "Frank, you're huge!"

"Yeah, seriously. Dude, you're enormous," says Darryl.

"Hey, guys, hang on a minute," I say, and I know they can tell that I'm completely serious. "Is Mom . . . still . . ." I can't seem to get my words out.

"Is she still alive? Heck yeah! Come on," says Darlene. "Let's go find her."

Then I notice we're about to be joined by three more ducks. It's Derrick, Dennis, and Dexter again.

"Okay, goose," says Derrick. "We did what you said. Time to get moving."

Clearly they still don't know who I am.

"Yeah, goose," says Dexter. "Five against one. Time to beat it. Darryl and Darlene, you guys can help us chase him off."

"I have no intention . . ." Darlene starts swimming at the other three, but I hold out my wing and stop her.

"I'll handle this," I say. I swim slowly toward Derrick, Dennis, and Dexter, and they start backing up. "I guess you guys don't remember me. I'm back from my quest, and I'd like to ask you some questions."

"F . . . F . . . Frank?" sputters Derrick. "We didn't mean . . . We shouldn't have . . ."

By now they're swimming backward as fast as they can. I put my neck in a curve and my head down because I'm in attack mode.

"Ahhh!" they scream, and turn to fly off. But Derrick isn't fast enough. I grab his tail feathers in my beak. I jerk and pull and swing my head back and forth while he keeps flapping to get away.

"Help!" Derrick calls to his friends, who are long gone by now.

Finally I feel his tail feathers release in my beak.

"Ouch!" Derrick yelps. But he can tell he's free now, and he flies off in a big hurry.

I swim back to Darryl and Darlene with three big tail feathers in my mouth and spit them out one by one. "Those are the best, most satisfying amulets I've ever collected."

"What was that all about?" says Darlene.

"Long story," I say. "I'll tell you all about it sometime."

"We can't go see Mom yet," I say. "We still have an urgent fox problem, right?"

They both nod. "And a lot of ducks didn't make it," says Darryl. "Remember Donna? The fox took her just two days ago."

"A lot of the duck clan has flown away. Only the ones with hatchlings are left, plus some stubborn folks," says Darlene.

"And you," I say.

"We didn't want to leave in case you came back," says Darlene.

"I'm sorry I left without saying goodbye," I say. "I was so mixed up. Anyway, we have a lot of catching up to do, but first can I introduce you to my friends?"

We swim over to the stream together. I can tell that my brother and sister are nervous . . . and naturally suspicious. When we walk up onto the bank, they look this way and that. When they see my friends, they seem very shy and tuck themselves in behind me. I step sideways so my friends can meet them. It reminds me of how Mom used to do the same thing with us.

I introduce Darryl and Darlene all around, and even though I save Flinch for last, they hardly take their eyes off him.

"And this is Flinch," I say finally.

"Very nice to meet you," says Flinch. "I . . . I don't eat eggs. Anymore." His front paws are rubbing like crazy, making me think he's nervous too.

"Flinch is one of my best friends," I say. I try to think of something that will make Darryl and Darlene relax. "I saved him from drowning after we got caught in a forest fire. Then he helped me a lot."

"Because I wanted to repay your brother for his kindness," says Flinch.

Darryl slowly turns his head to me. "You were in a forest fire?"

"I'll tell you everything someday," I say. "But listen,

we're going to try to get rid of the fox, and we have a plan. But we need you two."

"Not try," says Flinch. "We're going to do it!" He shoves a paw in the air. I can tell that Darryl and Darlene don't know what to think.

"Okay," I say. "But we really need everyone to learn their part."

I explain the plan. No one interrupts me, and when I'm done, I can't tell if my brother and sister are convinced. There is an awkward pause.

"Are you guys on board?" Mini finally asks.

Darryl and Darlene look at each other, and I think about how sudden and strange all this must seem to them. But then Darlene nods to Darryl, and Darryl breaks the silence. "We're in, Brother," he says. "We're family and we're all in!"

"Great!" I say. I want to cheer and honk really loudly and do a little dance, but I stay under control. "Mini, go see if the fox is on the hunt yet." Mini whirrs off.

"Flinch, go look out for Mini and tell us when she's coming. Let's go over the plan one more time while we're waiting," I say. I review it again with Darryl and Darlene and TR, and then we just wait. At first the silence is awkward, but then Darlene comes over and leans on me. I settle to the ground to make it easier, and then Darryl sits down near us and nibbles at the feathers on my neck. The feeling of family is something I didn't know I missed so much.

"She's coming!" Flinch says, scampering back toward us. "Mini's coming!"

Mini flits into the center of the group and lands on the ground, where she hops back and forth in a frenzy. "Okay, okay," she chirps. Her voice is even more shrill than usual. "He's coming. . . . I mean he's there. . . . I mean he's almost there. He's hiding and watching behind some tall grass."

"Okay, guys, does everyone remember their places and their jobs?" I look around. Nodding heads everywhere. But no one looks as nervous as my brother and sister. "Don't worry, guys, it's going to be okay." I try to sound more confident than I feel.

Mini is gone in an instant. Flinch scuttles away before he remembers his partner and scuttles back. "Come on, TR! Hurry up!"

"This is me hurrying!" says TR.

I take to the air with Darryl and Darlene close behind. I gain enough altitude to know I won't be noticed on the ground. As the pond comes into view, I take it in. From above it isn't hard to spot the fox hiding behind the tall grass, where he can see everything. A clump of ducks are swimming near the middle of the pond. The problem is that they are drifting in the direction of the fox. All he has to do is wait till they get close enough for him to attack.

I slow down until my siblings fly up beside me. "Now is your moment. Darryl, don't forget you're very sick. Remember our playacting? Lots of just sitting on the bank at first and then lots of limping. Darlene, your hurt wing act is so the fox doesn't give up on getting an easy meal. We're counting on you guys."

They look scared, but Darryl peels off without a word and begins to descend toward the pond.

"Good luck," says Darlene, and then she follows close behind Darryl. A lot is depending on their sick duck act. Actually everything depends on it. I can only imagine what that must feel like.

Chapter 22

I watch Darryl land on the bank. He settles down in a resting position in the fox's line of sight. The plan depends on the fox making the right choice . . . or, from his point of view, the wrong one. Darlene settles in close by. She starts making a show of preening, lifting her wings high in the air and then spreading them out to catch the warmth of the sun. Darryl has his head down, feathers ruffled, not moving. He is obviously a sick, sick bird. I feel a swell of pride for my siblings playing their part so well, and it makes me think back to our playacting days as young ones. But they must be very scared.

I circle and watch closely. Sure enough, the fox shifts his position and moves so he is directly facing Darryl and Darlene.

What I wasn't counting on is my brother and sister catching the attention of the entire duck clan, who can see the fox too. A loud quacking and excited flapping erupts from the mass of yellow beaks and white feathers as they try to warn their friends.

The fox begins to creep closer, no longer hidden behind the tall grass. The quacking and flapping from the clan gets louder, as the danger is now in plain sight. Two or three of the bigger ducks dash forward in a moment of courage before losing their nerve and returning to the safety of the group. The danger is so real, it is all I can do not to honk out a warning myself. But the plan is falling into place exactly right, even though it feels so wrong.

Suddenly the fox springs into action with terrifying quickness, and in a flash he cuts in half the gap between himself and his prey. Darlene flies upward and then back down.

With one wing dragging along the ground, she distracts the fox, and he runs a few steps in her direction. Darryl has hardly moved. I can't believe how brave he is. For a moment the fox looks confused. He lunges at Darlene, but she suddenly regains the use of her wings and flies up out of reach. The fox turns his attention back to Darryl, who has still not moved. Perfect.

I fly lower to be in position when it is my turn.

Darryl stands up stiffly and starts to limp toward the water. The fox darts in again with his alarming quickness, and the lame duck jumps into the water just ahead of those sharp teeth. The fox plunges in after his easy prey.

At that moment, a rock near the edge of the pond suddenly develops a head and neck and feet. TR can strike out surprisingly fast when she doesn't have to move her entire body. Just as she latches on to the fox's tail, another dark shape, a raccoon, springs out of a clump of grass and leaps onto the fox's back.

The fox is clearly confused. But the sick duck is just out of reach, barely able to paddle. The fox makes one final swimming lunge at the struggling duck, almost catching Darryl's tail in his teeth when suddenly my brother recovers and darts away, half flying and half running on the water, sprinting to the safety of the clamoring ducks in the center of the pond.

Now the fox is furious. He turns his body in a circle, teeth flashing, to deal with the creatures on his tail and back that have slowed him down and stopped him from catching his prey. But then a small dark shadow, Mini, comes out of the blue and begins darting in and out, pecking at the fox's head and preventing him from concentrating on any one opponent.

The fox snaps his teeth at Mini as if he is snapping at a fly, with about the same amount of success. The little bird is far too quick. After each snap, she darts in and makes another strike with her sharp beak on the top of the fox's head. All this time the raccoon is pulling and yanking on the fox's back fur. After sloshing around like this a little longer, the fox decides he has had enough and begins to paddle back to shore, ducking his head under the water every time the bird strikes, clearly having to work extra hard with two heavy animals on his back and tail.

This is my moment. The fox is tired and frustrated. I fold my wings and put myself into a sharp dive. With a long, loud honk at the very last moment to warn off Mini, I crash my body full force into the fox's head. He goes under.

It is too much to hope that this could be the end of the fox. But if I can just daze him, keep his head under water long enough . . . I seek out the top of the fox's head with my webbed feet and paddle his sharp, pointy nose as hard as I can. When the fox finally manages to break the surface to take a breath, I donk him with my beak and pummel him with my wings.

As long as I can keep up the barrage before the fox can swim to a spot shallow enough to find his footing, we have a chance. But we are losing the battle. The fox ignores my attacks on his head and just swims as hard as he can for land.

But then the most unexpected thing happens. The world is suddenly transformed into an explosion of white feathers. There are ducks everywhere, and they are all attacking the predator in the water. I'm pushed aside. Some of the ducks donk the fox's head and nose; others fly on his back to weigh him down.

It is an all-out effort to not allow him to reach shore. And it is working. There is a choking, raspy sound in the fox's throat as he struggles to swim. His head is getting lower and lower in the water.

I push my way back into the fight to get in my own blows to the fox's head. But I can tell the instant his feet touch down on solid ground. As soon as the fox's shoulders rise above the water, I know that the mission is finished.

The ducks seem to know it too. Once on land, one bite with those sharp teeth to a soft, feathery neck and it would be all over. I feel a sting of failure in my stomach. As the ducks stream away from the fox and back into the water, only one fighter seems to not understand that the battle is done.

"I got him!" shrieks Flinch. "I'm going to strangle him!" Somehow, in the confusion, the raccoon has managed to move up to the fox's neck. He is reaching as far around as he can, and his tiny paws are sunk into the fur.

"Flinch!" I shout. "It's over. Let go!"

It's clear that Flinch will never let go on his own, so I step up just as the fox gets completely out of the water and grab my friend by the neck with my beak and pull him off.

Then I remember how Flinch hates to let go of his enemies once he latches on. But he seems to understand this time, and as soon as the fox's tail clears the water, Flinch drops heavily to the ground. The fox turns and stares at the collection of animals in front of him. Water streams off his fur, making puddles on the ground. He looks smaller than before. He takes a step forward. None of us back away.

The fox lifts his lips and tries to growl, but the only thing that comes out is a bubbly gurgle. Water streams out of his nose. He shakes himself and then lowers his head. I lift myself up to my full height and arch my neck. To my surprise, I am bigger and taller than the fox. He takes a step back. I open my wings to seem even bigger, and that's all it takes. The fox turns around and slumps away into the tall grass. Mini gives him one final peck on the head.

It's over.

✺⫷ Chapter 23 ⫸✺

I stand on the ground where I faced the fox and stare into the tall grass where my enemy disappeared. Mini comes and lands on the grass in front of me. "You can fold up your wings up and stand down, Warrior Bird," she says.

I didn't even notice my wings were still outstretched, and I slowly do as Mini suggested. I know she is just teasing me, but it feels good anyhow to be called Warrior Bird, especially from Mini, who is the best warrior bird I've ever known.

"Do you think he'll be back?" I don't look down at Mini, but I know she is there.

"Predators hunt easy prey. That's why they go after sick animals," she says. "We just proved we're not easy prey. I don't think he'll be back anytime soon."

I turn around slowly and realize for the first time that everyone is staring at me, including the whole duck clan. Everyone except for TR, who is heading for a juicy clump of grass. Flinch is squeezing water off of his fur. "That fox was dead meat if you hadn't pulled me off him," he says. "He's lucky he can still breathe after these paws got ahold of him."

I'm about to say something about how small Flinch's

paws are compared with a fox's neck, but I decide to let it go. "You did great, Flinch," I say. The ducks are all gathered on the bank looking at me as if they expect me to speak. Only I can't think of anything. Then a duck separates herself from the group and walks toward me.

"Mom?" My heart feels so suddenly big and tight that it might stop beating. I sprint to her, remembering at the last minute to slow down so I don't knock her over. Then I have no idea what to do. She was always bigger than me, and now . . .

"Bring your head down here, Frank," she says. "I can't even reach your neck."

I sit on the ground in front of her and lower my neck. She nibbles the top of my head, and in an instant I'm five days old again and under Mom's protection. I nuzzle her back because I don't want her to ever stop.

"Frank," Mom says, "I missed you so much from the moment I found you had gone. I wish you would have told me you were leaving. I need you to come home right this minute and tell me everything that's happened to you."

I lift my head back up because in an instant I don't feel five days old anymore. "Mom, there is no way I can fit in your nest. Have you noticed how huge I am?"

She laughs her silvery laugh that I know so well. "Well, that doesn't mean you can't still tell me everything. Bring your friends with you."

I look up because I suddenly know what to say. "Hang on, Mom," I say, and I stand up and clear my throat. "Hey, everybody, maybe you remember me. I'm Frank and I'd like to introduce you to my friends."

Some of the ducks look at each other. Some of them pretend that there is a feather out of place and bend their necks around to "fix" it.

"But first I should say," I make my voice louder because it seems like no one is listening. "We should all be very, very proud of ourselves." No one is looking at me. "We were fighters in the face of extreme danger and we . . . all of us couldn't have done it without each other. This is my good friend Mini. She is the original fighter bird. And this is TR."

Mom is gazing at me and I can tell she is proud. It catches me off guard because I remember in a flash that this is what I always wanted. Darryl and Darlene have come up to stand with Mom, but some of the ducks are slipping into the water and starting to paddle away. I'm confused. Don't they care that we did this as a team? Don't they want to say thank you?

"And this is Flinch," I say louder.

Flinch raises up one nervous paw and waves. But at the mention of my raccoon friend there is a definite murmur in the crowd, and the remaining ducks turn to swim away.

"He's a raccoon, but he doesn't eat eggs." I'm yelling now because all I can see is duck tails.

"Eggs, yuck!" says Flinch. "I hate eggs!"

I stare at Flinch because I know for a fact that this is not true. But I love him even more for saying it, even if it isn't going to do any good. He looks at me, puts his front paws up, and shrugs.

I watch the flock of ducks get smaller and smaller. No one turns around to look back. No one says thank you. No one seemed glad to see me. Mom and Darryl and Darlene are the only ducks left. I feel a deep sadness run through me like a river. But there is another feeling inside me, something I can't explain. I try to figure it out, but it doesn't come to me.

I shake my head to clear my thoughts. "Mom," I say. "I'd like to introduce you to my friends: Flinch, Mini, and TR. TR, please stop eating and come over here and meet my mom."

"It's very nice to meet all of you." Mom nods to each one of them. "Thank you so much for everything you did for us today."

"Darryl and Darlene, you guys were fantastic," I say. "We couldn't have pulled it off without you. Weren't they great, Mom?"

"I was terrified when I saw that Darryl was sick and about to be eaten," says Mom. "Why didn't you tell me about your plan?"

"It was complicated, Mom," I say.

"I'll never forgive you for not saying goodbye," she says.

"Mom!" I say, and she looks up at me. "Yes, you will."

I turn back to Darryl and Darlene. "You should head back to the pond. Otherwise everyone will give you a hard time."

Darlene steps up to me and I lower myself to the ground. We rub necks just like the old days.

"Are you leaving?" she says.

"I think I'd better," I say. "You guys will always be my

first family and I'll always love you. But it isn't going to work for me to live here."

Saying this makes me want to lay my long neck out on the ground and never get up. I had always hoped, in a small, secret place in my heart, that I could make it right . . . make it so the ducks would like me, make it so this could be my home. That part of me has gone dark.

"Anyway," I say, "I have to go figure out how to be a goose, and I have these really great friends to help me out when I mess up too bad."

Darryl steps up. "I want to be one of your really great friends too," he says. "Plus I'm gonna really give everyone a talking to. I can't believe how they just turned around and never said thank you or anything."

I put a wing over my brother's back. "No one is more important to me than you and Mom and Darlene," I say. "But the main thing I want for you is to go back to the clan and be the best, happiest duck you can be."

"Are you sure you can't stay?" says Darlene.

"Yes, stay," says Mom. "Stay and teach everyone how you can be a goose and still be family."

I shake my head. "I'm not ready to be anyone's teacher," I say. "I'm not sure I can do that . . . especially here."

"Come back sometimes and visit?" says Darlene.

"Of course," I say.

"I love you, Brother," says Darlene.

"Yeah, me too," says Darryl.

They both come and reach up to rub my neck. Then they both slip into the pond and give me a wave before they swim away.

"Mom," I say, and then I look up when I remember we're not alone. Mini is staring at us, but she quickly starts preening under her left wing. TR has hauled herself over to a fresh clump of grass, and Flinch is checking himself for ticks.

"Mom," I say again. "You hatched me out and I'm so thankful you gave me my life. I remember all of your lessons. You taught me so much—"

"About how to be a duck," she interrupts me. "I'm so sorry I couldn't teach you how to be a goose."

I take a deep breath. "Yeah, that was pretty confusing," I say. "But I'll figure it out. You gave me love, so I'm pretty sure that makes you the best mom ever."

And that's when I remember the feeling that was missing when the flock swam away without saying welcome back or thank you: loneliness. Even in the face of my whole duck extended family turning away from me, I don't feel lonely. My mom still loves me, and I have this crazy bunch of friends who are almost like . . . a new family.

"I'll love you and worry about you every day that you're gone," she says. "I wish I had an amulet to give you."

Amulets, I think to myself. I'm finished with amulets.

All I need are a few friends to go into battle with. But I don't say anything. I needed love too, and Mom gave me everything she had.

"No, don't worry about me, Mom," I say. "I'm huge now. I can take on a fox and win! Plus, I have my friends."

"Nothing you can say makes me worry any less, but I understand that you need to go. Come back often," she says, and reaches up as high as she can. I lower my head so she can give my head one last nibble. And suddenly the sadness of saying goodbye to my mom—and to my old self—begins to overwhelm me. I slowly straighten up.

"I love you forever, Mom, but I'd better say goodbye now." I say.

She slips into the pond and swims away.

I turn to my friends, who are all watching me now. "You guys were fantastic and the best friends ever. Thanks for everything!"

"What, you're leaving us too?" says Mini.

"Yeah, I thought we were like your new family." says Flinch. "We gotta stick together. So, where are we going?"

"I didn't say I was leaving," I say.

"Sounded like it to me," says TR, who for once isn't eating.

"So where are we going?" says Flinch.

No one says anything for a moment, but everyone is looking at me.

"I was thinking I might need to learn how to migrate," I say. "Do you guys want to try migrating?"

"Yeah . . . no," says Flinch. "That sounds a little too goosey for me."

"I'm going to stay right here at the duck pond," says TR. "I've been hurried along on quests and journeys enough to last me for a long while."

This surprises me. "Here with the ducks who were so mean to you last time?" I say.

"If they bother me, I'll just bite a duck tail, and I won't let go until they promise to leave me alone. You're not the only one who learned something on the quest." TR walks slowly over to a new clump of grass and yanks out a bite to start chewing.

"What about you, Mini?" I say.

She tips her head to one side. "Might be time to build a nest and start a new family."

I nod slowly, and I know she's thinking about her last family. "Good luck," I say. "Your babies will be so lucky to have a mom like you." Then I turn to the group. Everyone except TR is looking at me. "And good luck to everyone. I'll never ever forget you and everything you did for me." Feelings of excitement and sadness begin to overwhelm me, and I can't find any more words.

"You'd *better* not forget us," says Mini.

"Yeah," says Flinch. "We're gonna miss you like crazy.

You saved my life, and anyhow, I hardly even remember my life without you."

"Flinch," I say, "saving you might have been the best thing I ever did. So now you go off back to your life, and I'll try to learn how to be a goose." I walk over and nibble the top of his fuzzy head. "And when we get together again we'll share our stories. Deal?"

"Deal," says Flinch.

"But no eating eggs, okay?" I say.

"Never!" says Flinch, and he puts a paw over his heart.

TR gulps down her last swallow. "Promise you won't stay away too long," she says.

I look down at her. It might be the first tender thing I've heard her say. "TR," I say, "you are my first best friend. I will never forget you, and I will always find you. I wouldn't have lasted a single day in the forest without you."

"Bye, everyone, I love you forever," I say. I feel as though if I don't take to the sky and start flying I might dissolve in a puddle of sadness. A breeze suddenly brushes in and ruffles my feathers. Turning to face that sign, I open my wings and let it lift me up. I flap strongly and rise quickly into a sky that is blue and cloudless and looks as if it goes on forever.

I look down one more time and my group, my friends, are all looking up. Mini and Flinch are waving.

"Bye, everyone," I say again, my voice sounding like the

moon. I hope they can hear me. I close my eyes for a moment and let the wind slip over my wings. Then, listening to a tiny, soft voice in my head that I've never listened to before, I turn and head in a brand-new direction.

Acknowledgments

More than anyone, I want to thank my sister, Janie, whose unexpected belief in me sparked a world of possibility. I also want to thank my writing buddies Mark Friel and Tom Birdseye for their time, skills, and insights to help this book come together.

About the Author

Chris Kurtz is a teacher, storyteller, and the author of the award-winning *Adventures of a South Pole Pig*. He is also the author of *The Pup Who Cried Wolf* and has cowritten picture books with his sister Jane Kurtz. He lives in Portland, Oregon, with his family.